Writing Box

The Writing Box

ALLISON ALI

To Jillian

TOBAGO
Charlotteville
Castara
Plymouth
Moriah
Roxborough
Canaan
Scarborough
CARIBBEAN SEA
VENEZUELA
Macuro
Puerto de Hierro
Dragon's Mouth
Chaguaramas
San Juan
Port of Spain
Tunapuna
Arima
Valencia
ANDREW
Maracas
Blanchisseuse
Matelot
Toco
Galera Point
ATLANTIC OCEAN
Sangre Grande
Manzanilla
Chaguanas
Talparo
CARONI
Gulf of Paria
Couva
Tabaquite
NARIVA
TRINIDAD
Rio Claro
Guayaro Point
San Fernando
La Brea
Brighton
Point Fortin
ST. PATRICK
Debe
Penal
Princes Town
Tableland
VICTORIA
MAYARO
Pierreville
Guayaguayare
Galeota Point
Fullarton
San Francique
Siparia
Basse Terre
Moruga
Serpent's Mouth
VENEZUELA

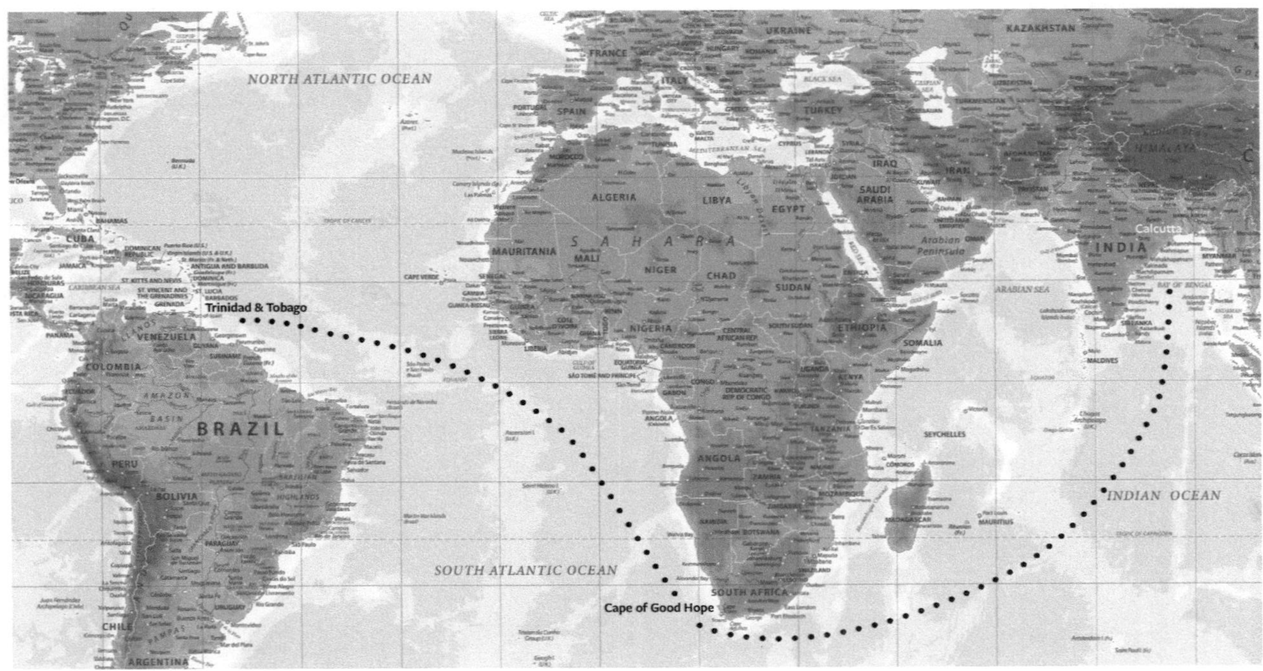

NORTH ATLANTIC OCEAN
SOUTH ATLANTIC OCEAN
INDIAN OCEAN
Trinidad & Tobago
Cape of Good Hope
Calcutta
FRANCE
SPAIN
PORTUGAL
ITALY
UKRAINE
KAZAKHSTAN
TURKEY
IRAQ
IRAN
SAUDI ARABIA
EGYPT
LIBYA
ALGERIA
MAURITANIA
MALI
NIGER
CHAD
SUDAN
NIGERIA
ETHIOPIA
SOMALIA
ANGOLA
ZAMBIA
TANZANIA
KENYA
SOUTH AFRICA
BOTSWANA
MOZAMBIQUE
MADAGASCAR
SEYCHELLES
MAURITIUS
COMOROS
INDIA
SRI LANKA
MALDIVES
CUBA
JAMAICA
PANAMA
COLOMBIA
VENEZUELA
GUYANA
SURINAME
BRAZIL
PERU
BOLIVIA
PARAGUAY
CHILE
URUGUAY
ARGENTINA
ECUADOR
SAHARA
AMAZON BASIN
PAMPAS
Arabian Peninsula
Libyan Desert
CARIBBEAN SEA
MEDITERRANEAN SEA
BLACK SEA
RED SEA
ARABIAN SEA
BAY OF BENGAL
CAPE VERDE
SENEGAL
GAMBIA
GUINEA-BISSAU
SIERRA LEONE
LIBERIA
CÔTE D'IVOIRE
GHANA
TOGO
BENIN
CAMEROON
GABON
CONGO
DEMOCRATIC REP OF CONGO
CENTRAL AFRICAN REP.
SOUTH SUDAN
UGANDA
NAMIBIA
SWAZILAND
ST. KITTS AND NEVIS
ANTIGUA AND BARBUDA
DOMINICA
ST. LUCIA
BARBADOS
ST. VINCENT AND THE GRENADINES
GRENADA
HONDURAS
NICARAGUA
COSTA RICA
SÃO TOMÉ AND PRINCIPE
EQUATORIAL GUINEA
TROPIC OF CANCER
TROPIC OF CAPRICORN
EQUATOR
HIMALAYA
MYANMAR
Bermuda (U.K.)
Puerto Rico (U.S.)
Azores (Port.)
Madeira Islands (Port.)
Canary Islands (Sp.)
St. Helena (U.K.)
Tristan da Cunha Group (U.K.)

"... it soothes me better to shape out some tale from my own heart, more near akin to my own passions and habitual thoughts ... and beguile myself with trust that mellower years will bring a riper mind and clearer insight ..."

—*Wordsworth*

ONE

———

ON A PRE-DAWN MORNING in July, a fleet of low stratus clouds settled over the slumbering town of Everly shrouding it in a misty rain. The moon not full-faced, but a sliver, like the curve of an ear, cast a muted lunar light on the draped and shuttered windows of the two-storied homes. The town sat fifty miles outside of New York City.

But before it was a town, it was a woodland of a hundred acres. It had a pond on the north side and was home to a family of dabbling mallard ducks. A pair of weeping willows graced the bank of the pond. On windy days, it was full of sound and movement. The spindly pine trees swayed and nodded while their leaves rustled and chattered. The long fronds of the willow trees bobbed up and down in the pond like curtsying ballerinas.

The woodland was owned by John C. Peyton, an engineer and private art collector. He lived in a large brick and limestone house with his wife Everly. To their disappointment, they had no children. Some years later, when his wife died, he cut down part of the woodland and built a town.

He named the streets after the trees, and the town after his wife, Everly. The firehouse was on Ash Street. The library, the bank, the post office, the supermarket, and the gym were on Laurel Drive. The railroad, Everly Station, ran between Beech and Cypress Streets. Every morning, except on Saturdays and Sundays, the first eastbound train to the city left the station at 6:13a.m.

Eighteen miles away, at John F. Kennedy International Airport, a Caribbean Airlines flight BW (*pronounced Bee-Wee*) #7950 was scheduled for take-off at 6:13a.m headed for Trinidad and Tobago.

All was still and quiet in the town of Everly, except at 296 Willow Street. It was the home of the Kilmere family, Ana, Peter and their fifteen-year-old daughter, Julia.

Light seeped out of Julia's bedroom on the second floor. An unzipped, half-stuffed backpack laid on the bed with a open suitcase beside it.

Julia padded back and forth between her bedroom and bathroom packing her toiletries in the suitcase. She had a flight to catch in less than three hours.

She was mumbling a mental checklist when she heard her mother's voice from below and stopped.

"Julia! Hurry darling, you'll miss your flight," Ana called.

"Coming mom!" Julia said

She quickly finished packing. Zipped up her luggage, scanned the room and headed out the door.

Her mother waited for her at the foot of the stairs. Were her eyes wet, Julia wondered.

"Whose idea was it to let you get on a plane by yourself at fifteen?" Ana asked.

"Oh mom, don't look so sad. You and dad will be there in three weeks. Then we fly back home together. The time will go by fast. You'll see," Julia reassured her mother. Hoping all the while she couldn't hear the excitement in her voice.

Every year in July, Ana and Julia took a flight to Trinidad so Julia could spend part of her summer vacation with Ana's mother, Adhari Perla. Her mother would spend the day and fly out the next morning back to New York. Three weeks later, her parents came to Trinidad to spend a week before all three, Julia and her parents, flew back to New York.

But this was the first time she would take the trip to Trinidad alone.

She trudged downstairs dragging her carry-on behind her, the spinner wheels *twacking* on every riser.

Her mother took the stairs, two at a time, to rescue it and her ears from the beating the wheels took.

"I know," Ana picked back up the conversation, "it's just this is the first time you're flying there without us." She turned to Julia then quickly looked away to hide her anxious stare.

"Where's dad?" Julia asked.

"Waiting in the car. It's drizzling outside so be careful on the path," her mother cautioned.

They shuffled out the car. Her mother threw her suitcase in the open trunk as Julia slipped in the backseat shrugging off her backpack on the seat beside her. Her mother shut the trunk and came round to the front.

"Have everything?" her father asked, looking at her through the rearview mirror.

"Yes, I think so," Julia hesitantly replied as she did a quick mental check. Then nodded to indicate mental check is over and she is certain she has everything.

"Here's hoping there's no traffic at this time of the morning," he announced, grabbing Ana's headrest to look back as he reversed onto the street. He didn't trust his back-up camera especially when the streetlights were dimmed from the rain.

"Don't forget to call us when you arrive," her mother reminded her. "Did you remember to pack sunscreen?"

"Yes mom." She wished she could text her best friend, Samantha but didn't want to wake her.

". . . you're not a native. You don't look like them. So you can't wander off on your own." Her father said as she caught the tail end of it.

"Wait, what?" she asked.

"I said, just because we go every summer, it doesn't make you a local. You may think that you are, but they do not." Her father explained.

"What does that mean?" Julia asked.

"It means you still need to be careful and only go places with people you know," her father said with the "this is not a suggestion" tone.

Peter, a writer, unlike her mother had different tones. His firm and straight to the point tone, like it was now, meant the matter was settled. He used it if he sensed either her or her mother, Ana was making a choice that could put them in danger. But most of the time, he had a light teasing tone, except when he was working on a book. During those times, his characters became so real to him, he would say he was merely writing the conversations they had. When someone asked him a question, there was often a long pause before he answered, as though he was being summoned from a distant land.

When they pulled into terminal four at JFK airport, Peter inched his way to the curb. With the car idling, he jumped out to help Julia with her luggage while she said goodbye to her mother.

Her mother seized the moment to whisper some advice, "don't forget, always stay with grams or at least, with Kavita and the kids."

Julia nodded, "I know mom," wanting to reassure her mother just as much as herself. She turned to her father.

"Thanks dad. I got it from here," she said.

"See you soon Jules," Peter said giving her a hug and a kiss on her forehead.

She pulled up the handle off her carry-on and headed inside. She turned and gave a last wave. They waved back and then pulled off, easing into the flow of traffic.

TWO

———

J ULIA CROSSED THE AIRPORT'S threshold from local to traveler with ease although this would be her first flight without her parents' permanent presence. For her, it just meant she had to pay more attention. She knew all airports were not created equal. As a child, when they traveled as a family, her father taught her what airport jargon meant. Words used in the context of air travel such as delay, terminal and departure would mean something entirely different in, for example, her mother's clinical world.

John F. Kennedy (JFK) International Airport, renamed after the thirty-fifth president, was formerly Idlewild Airport and before that, Jamaica Sea-Airport when it was just a landing strip on a large marshland in Jamaica Bay.

The JFK international airport had six working terminals, one hundred and twenty-eight gates, four runways, and an AirTrain, a passenger system used to connect the pedestrian world to the airport.

Julia headed for the Caribbean Airlines ticket counter inside T4 or terminal four. She quickly spotted an empty kiosk and hurried to it instead of the serpentine line. Checked-in and made her way to the even longer TSA security line.

While waiting her turn, she looked around and marveled at the hub of activity this early in the morning. She noticed the pace of the people around her. The staff at the counter slapped smiles and luggage tags, their eyes trained on the person in front of them. The TSA workers, unsmiling and watchful, had their eyes trained on the monitors. The frequent fliers walked with a familiar, but disenchanted air as they made their way to the bar, airport lounge or boarding so they can tuck back into their phones.

Julia paid more attention to those in transit as she related more to them. She noticed who the travelers were—executives and families. The few who were traveling solo were adults. She was the only teenager flying alone. This realization settled around the edges of her mind. She felt both nervous and thrilled. She knew the flight attendants would keep an eye on her, but she wished her mother was there.

In the past, she could listen to music and just trail behind her parents who walked way too fast for her at airports. She now knew why. T4 was a mile long with forty-eight gates, and depending on where her gate was, she would have to hurry. After she cleared security, she grabbed a vacant bench to sit on to lace up her sneakers then bolted off to find gate A2. She got there with enough time to buy a bottle of water from the closest Hudson News stand, then the boarding call came.

She boarded the plane, shuffling up the narrow aisle, as wide as a mountain ridge, to locate her seat about midway down the plane. She found it, her row of three seats were empty. She quickly dropped her backpack on the aisle seat to hoist her carry-on over her head to stow it, wheels first, in the overhead bin. She was keenly aware of the line of passengers behind her waiting. She scooted past the two empty seats in her row and plopped down on hers by the acrylic window. She grabbed her backpack and folded her body to wrangle it into the fourteen inches of space underneath the seat in front of her. A flight staff stopped by to ask if she needed any help. She tilted her head and shot a smile of gratitude, "I got it", thank you though" she said as she continued to jostle it into place. She finished, straightened up and snapped in the metal buckle around her waist. She knew from the time she entered the airport, her being a minor, she could ask for assistance from any of the airport staff and even now, on the plane, from the flight crew, but she hadn't yet learned their usefulness. She wanted to take this flight solo and to navigate this journey on her own as much as possible. It was a small test she had devised for herself. She wanted to know how well and how much she had learned just by watching her parents navigate the world of travel.

For a while, she watched how the other passengers stowed their luggage, settled into their seats, and prepared themselves for the four-hour flight. Some had a bustling, noisy manner, as they jostled and bumped their way up the aisle to find their seat and stow their luggage, with every effort making their presence known and noticed.

While others had a quiet, fluid, and practiced manner about them as they navigated the forty-three-centimeter-wide aisle with ease, pausing briefly to hoist their carry-on, wheels first, in the overhead bin to then tuck into their seats.

Julia cast her mind back to when she traveled with her parents, whose flying habits were more like the latter's practiced and efficient. She stifled a yawn as it was still early morning. It was a four-hour flight with no Wi-Fi, so she sank into her seat, pulled her hoodie over her head, and won-dered who would sit beside her.

Her mind, like fingers outstretched to grasp a wayward whisp, reached to pull back to the front of her mind the words her mother ever so casually whispered to her earlier—"or at least with Kavita and the kids." Honey-brown eyes, straight nose and full mouth sailed into her vision—Jonathan. She shook her head to think of something else.

Did her mother somehow know or guess about her secret crush on auntie Kavita's eldest, Jona-than? He was seventeen with sapodilla brown skin and light brown eyes.

She thought it was the strangest thing that out of nowhere she began to care if he liked the way she did her hair or the outfit she wore. When in the past, she barely gave him a second thought since they grew up around each other as far back as she could recall.

Their mothers were best friends since primary school. But last year something changed when she came to the island for the summer.

Her best friend, Samantha, had come with her. It was the first time she had been allowed to invite a friend. So naturally, she asked if Samantha could come. Her parents gave their permission. Then all that Spring they talked about the island, the heat, the beaches, the spicy foods and Jonathan and his sisters.

By the time Samantha arrived, it was as though she knew them already. Except, they did not know her. But what Julia was not prepared for was Samantha's reaction when she actually came face-to-face with Jonathan. Julia couldn't understand why her friend started to act so weird. All the things Samantha had said she would not be interested in doing, she was now ready to do it if Jonathan suggested it.

She, Samantha, Jonathan and his two younger sisters, Nalini and Shoba, spent most of the summer together. But it was something in the way Samantha would look at Jonathan with her head tilted to the side, her eyes resting lazily on his face that made Julia feel invisible, like she was no longer there or should be there. Nothing was ever said between Samantha and Jonathan to confirm Julia's feelings. If anything, Jonathan seemed oblivious to her. What bothered Julia more was why it should irk her if Samantha and Jonathan liked each other.

On the fringes of her consciousness, she was beginning to admit to herself that Jonathan mattered to her, and she wanted more than friendship. Maybe this was why she didn't tell Samantha about this trip for fear that she might ask to come. Or worse, ask her if she was interested in him. She wasn't ready for those kinds of questions.

She would keep this to herself. It would be her secret. Like the other secret hidden in the attic of her mind. In the grand scheme of things, she knew if someone found out she had a crush on a childhood friend, it might illicit a nod or smile. But if anyone ever found out about her other secret, well, she feared it might change the way they looked at her, or even spoke to her.

She never understood why someone would entrust another person with their secrets, then forbid the person from telling anyone -evidently a feat they themselves failed at.

But she had another reason. She did not consider it a secret as much as an inner knowing she possessed, not at her birth, fifteen years ago, but some years later.

She must have been around nine years old when she became aware of her separateness from her mother. She still felt that she was a member, not of her mother's body, like a limb or a leg, but a member of a family. Yet, it dawned on her that she was a separate person from them. She had her own thoughts and feelings.

She remembered the day the idea was formed. It was a Sunday afternoon in the winter. It was snowing lightly outside. She was in the living room with her parents. She and her father sat Indian style across each other on the living room carpet playing a game of Scrabble while her mother reclined on the sofa reading a medical journal.

While her father concentrated on his seven tiles, his brows furrowed as he chewed on his lower lip, she studied her mother's profile as though looking at a sculpture at the museum. She looked at each feature on its own, not as part of her whole face and was fascinated that while her face had a rounded softness, her mother had almond shaped eyes, cheekbones pronounced and high like small mountain peaks, and thin lips.

Then she did the same with her father, looking at his features to find the similarities to her own face. She noticed his green eyes, the color of a new leaf, with streaks of honey gold. She had inherited the golden-brown flecks in her eyes. His nose was straight. His lashes long reminding her of a gi-raffe, the thought had made her burst into giggles. He swept his gaze up towards her and asked her, "What?"

"Nothing, it's just that you're a writer and you're struggling to make a word with seven let-ters," she deflected.

"I'm staring at a bunch of vowels. I could make a word -in French" was his reply.

"Nah ah, you know the rules. Only English words I can ask Google," she had said. He spoke three languages, so she made him stick to the rule of only English.

It was during that ordinary domestic scene, she realized she was separate from them. She could also look at the way she lived and felt grateful that she had both her parents living in the same house with her, who loved and cared for her every need. She thought then and there that her life was perfect. Her little world and the people in it, her parents, her grandmother, even her best friend Samantha was all she needed. And there is nothing that would destroy her perfect world. But she had to keep it to herself, she had to keep it a secret. She couldn't post about it or give it a hashtag. She was afraid if anyone found out they might think she walked around thinking she was better than everyone, which wasn't how she felt.

As she grew older, although she maintained her belief in her perfect life, she knew the world at large was not perfect and it saddened her to think of anyone not having what she had, like Agnes from art class at school.

Agnes sat at the back of the class. Her desk was near a wall of single pane windows with eastern exposures. Art class was the first class on Tuesdays and Thursdays. She would be the first one there, sitting quietly with her eyes fixed on some point outside towards the open soccer field until Mrs. Avery, the art teacher, started class. It was as though her singular goal was to make herself as invisible as the spidery crack on the seventh window.

Agnes had two dresses. She wore them at the same time, one over the other. The students teased her about it, "Hey Aggie, you couldn't decide which one to wear this morning, yeah I have that same problem, or did you get dress in the dark?" then they cackled with laughter as they walked away. She would roll her eyes and ignore them.

One dress was navy-blue with big yellow sun-flowers knitted on the front which she wore on Tuesdays and Thursdays perhaps because it was music and art classes on those days. The second dress was forest green with a pattern of black and white hexagonal shapes. She wore those on Mondays, Wednesdays, and Fridays which were math, science, and gardening days. On cold days, she wore black tights with rum-colored ankle boots, and on warm days she wore a pair of Birkenstock sandals.

It was a sunny morning in the fall when Julia first noticed Agnes. The spacious art room had tilted architect-style desks and a wall of windows with eastern exposures. Light poured in through the single pane windows casting shadows on Julia's drawing. She shifted when she sensed movement behind her.

She looked over her shoulder and saw a girl wearing a blue dress with sunflowers on it. She sat in the last row. She was drawing quietly, as they all were, but her concentrated quiet seemed to emit from within her.

Just then, the girl looked up and caught Julia staring at her. She seemed to quickly transform from being relaxed and at ease to nervous and agitated. As if by reflex, her chin sunk into her neck and her shoulders hiked up to cradle her ears. She looked like a stricken animal ready for flight. Julia thought if the girl was hoping for invisibility, like the spidery crack on the seventh window in class, she was doing a good job. She knew her name was Angie or maybe Agnes, she thought she heard the teacher say, although she couldn't remember exactly. Julia decided to look for an opportunity to talk to her.

A week later, as Julia was gathering her things, she looked up to see Agnes, she made it a point to remember her name the next time the teacher had called on her, standing in front of the flyer for the winter play.

"Thinking of signing up?" Julia asked casually. Agnes replied, "probably, you?" as she still faced forward.

"Yeah. I signed up already. Casting starts Friday after school," Julia couldn't help the excitement creeping into her nonchalant answer.

"Hey, we have music next, want to walk together?" Julia wanted to keep the conversation light, so she changed the subject.

Agnes smiled and nodded.

Over the next few months, Julia learned why Agnes wore only two dresses. She and her mother, Trudy, lived in a one-bedroom apartment in a women's shelter. Agnes's grandmother had made her those two dresses before she died so she treasured them. She and her mother were lucky to have their own apartment, but there were some challenges. Sometimes, there were unannounced inspections from management and one time, she came home from school and her headphones went missing. Agnes told Julia she did not tell her mother because she did not want to cause any trouble for them. But she knew that she needed to keep the things important to her with her.

It was the first time it dawned on Julia that not everyone had the same circumstances in life, who did not have what she took for granted. It made her more appreciative of what she had, but she was also proud of herself that she could still see people for who they were with their own intrinsic value which had nothing to do with what they had.

Nevertheless, it inspired in her a desire to share with others if she could. She told her mother about Agnes so when they made their annual school shopping list, it would include extra items for a special bag they would put together just for Agnes. The tricky part was always how she would give it to Agnes without making her think it was a handout.

THREE

———

"LADIES AND GENTLEMEN, we have begun our descent into Trinidad. Please turn off all portable electronic devices and stow them until we have arrived at the gate. In preparation for landing . . ." the pilot's announcement roused Julia from her nap.

She stifled a yawn as she stretched in her seat and flipped up the window shade to look out. She saw a sparkling emerald sea below with high swells of island pride tapering off to seek a long swath of sandy shores.

The island of Trinidad was thirty-eight miles wide off the north-east coast of Venezuela. In the sixteenth century, Spanish ships landed on Invaders Bay, three miles from the capital, Port of Spain in search of gold. They found, instead, two tribes of people, the Caribs and Arawaks. In time, they established cotton and sugar plantations.

Then late one February, two hundred years later, a fleet of eighteen long British warships were fast-approaching Port of Spain. They arrived, quickly seized control of the island, and turned it into a crown colony with a thriving plantation economy from the sweat of a slave society.

An average sugar plantation required eighty to a hundred and twenty laborers to plant, cut, cart, and crush the sugarcane. They used either water or horse-powered mills. After it was illegal to use free labor, they hired indentured workers from India. They sailed to Trinidad fastened to work contracts of either three or five years depending on if they were male or female.

Then one day, it all changed. Using neither coin nor cannon, the locals called *Trinis*, formed a political party, and used the tenor and timbre of their voices to vote the imperialist nation out of office and country. Julia's ancestors sailed on the one of those ships from the port of Kolkata to the Caribbean tied to a contract. And like many before them, they came and remained.

The Boeing 747 touched down, on the east-west runway at Piarco International Airport in Trinidad, under a white-hot sun. There was a short walk from the airplane to customs situated in an air-conditioned building with cathedral ceilings. Julia made her way through the North Terminal.

She spotted Mr. Patrick, the tall, barrel-chested customs officer who looked at ease fitted out in a narrow booth and joined his line. Julia's grandmother helped deliver his son Curtis. When it was her turn, she marched up to his booth matching his warm, wide grin.

"Julia, yuh back for yuh holiday to see yuh grannie eh girl?" asked Mr. Patrick in a thick sing-song accent.

"Yes, Mr. Patrick." She replied, handing him her blue passport.

"Wait, yuh by yuhself dis time?" He asked peering over her shoulder.

Julia's smile widened, her chest rose a little, "I fly solo from now," she declared.

"Ah ha, we getting big I see, auright. Well, it's good to see yuh and say hello to grannie for us." Mr. Patrick said stamping her passport.

"Will do. Thanks Mr. P!" said Julia and shuffled away. She loved how the locals would have a little lift to their voice at the end of a sentence to make it sound more like a dangling question than a statement.

She hurried through the concourse now as she knew her grandmother was out there in the throng of island brown faces waiting for her. The excitement built up inside of her to see her and be outside in the island, in the hot sun, and smells of food from the street food vendors. She just wanted to take it all in.

Then it suddenly dawned on her that perhaps her grandmother might not be there. What if her mother expected her to take a taxi to her grandmother's house as part of her first solo travel experience. She didn't even know the actual address of her grandmother's house except that it was situated in the northern range overlooking Maracas Bay and was called Ambar Taj which meant sky jewel.

At least one of the advantages of living on a small island, she reasoned, was that everyone knew her grandmother, Adhari Perla. So, she took a calming breath and felt confident she would figure it out.

Then she spotted her grandmother and broke out into a run, relieved and happy.

"Ri-Ri, you're finally here. Oh! let me look at you. You got taller," came the barrage of comments from her grandmother. Julia hadn't realized how much she grew, since her father was six feet tall, she always felt short standing next to him. But now, standing beside her grandmother, who reached her shoulders, she could see it now. Her grandmother was the only one who called her Ri-Ri since they shared the name Adhari.

"*Chalo*, let's go," said her grandmother. Before leaving the air-conditioned building, Julia pulled out a baseball cap from her backpack and slapped it on her head as they walked out.

"Grams how far away is the car?" asked Julia as she tucked flyaway strands under her cap.

"Not far, just a little walk," Adhari reassured.

"You drove by yourself?"

"Yes, it's daytime." Apparently, finding it a touchy subject, her grandmother asked, "are you hungry? We could stop at Sandy's roti shop on the way home?"

"No, thanks. I'm good," Julia replied.

They found the car after some time. Julia dropped her backpack on the backseat and then hopped into the front seat adjusting the vents towards her.

Her grandmother eased the car out the parking lot towards the boulevard, heading for the highway.

"How's your dad, RiRi?"

"Dad's good. He's working on a new book with a new editor," Julia replied.

Her grandmother nodded.

"Anything new grams?"

"Nothing much. The Sundars are having another baby. In fact, Kavita is due in another couple of weeks."

But Julia already knew that. Jonathan had told her about the baby. But for some reason, she was reluctant to let her family know they continued to talk even when she was in New York. She didn't know how they would react to their friendship, and she wasn't ready to find out.

As the car climbed the northern hills, the two-storied house slowly came into view sitting squarely on a hill overlooking the blue-green watery expanse below. It had a white gabled roof with a wraparound veranda.

Her grandmother had said when she and grandpa Kishon first saw it, they thought it looked as if it had tumbled out of the sky, so they decided to call it Ambar Taj, sky jewel.

They pulled up to the rear of the house. Julia jumped out and grabbed her backpack and carry-on. She wheeled it into the cool interior, stopping to remove her shoes before heading down the bedroom hallway.

Her grandmother followed behind.

"RiRi, do you want to rest a little and I will prepare lunch for when you wake up?"

"Yes grams that sounds good. Can I have a bottle of water please?"

"I put a few in your room. I know how the humidity makes you thirsty," her grandmother said.

"Thanks grams, you're the best. See you in a

little while," said Julia as she hoisted her carry-on on the bed. Then suddenly stopped and turned to say, "grams, I can't wait for tonight."

"What's tonight *beta*?" her grandmother crinkled her brow and asked.

"After dinner comes a story," Julia sang.

Her grandmother laughed, "Oh you know just the other day, I remembered a nice one about your mom when she was your age."

"No, grams, I love those stories, but not tonight. Tonight, I want to hear a story about the old times, the past. "Ive been reading some books on the history of the island. I want to hear those kinds of stories like how your grandparents came to the island and lived on a sugar plantation," Julia explained.

"Okay, we'll light the flambeaux to keep the mosquitos away, we'll make tea and sit on the veranda and tell you a nice, long story," her grandmother replied.

FOUR

———

LATER THAT EVENING, Julia woke up starving after an afternoon nap. Her grandmother was in the tiled kitchen standing at the counter near the stove. Her hands and rolling pin dusted with flour as she deftly rolled out the dough and then slapped it onto a *tawa* or thin skillet which sat on the stove over a low flame. The white lace curtains fluttered in the gentle breeze coming through the louvered windows.

Julia clapped her hands with happiness, startling her grandmother, when she saw the *paratha* roti, a soft and flaky pull apart bread, on the stove.

"Oh grams, you're making my favorite. What are we having it with?" Julia asked.

Her grandmother asked, "how long has it been since you had *baigan choka?*" The word baigan was Hindi for eggplant. This was a dish made by roasting eggplant on an open flame, scooping out the inside, then mashed with a drizzle of olive oil, then seasoned with salt, crushed garlic, and hot pepper. Julia quickly crossed to the counter to peek inside the covered dish.

"Too long, grams. You know mom doesn't make it like you. Where do you want me to set the table for dinner inside or out?"

"On the veranda please," Adhari requested.

Julia grabbed a basket and filled it like Noah's ark with a pair of everything, except silverware. They would eat with their hands.

From the living room through glass sliding doors, the covered veranda was more an extension of the inside brought outdoors. A cloth hammock hung from a hook on the side overlooking the road below. A pair of rocking chairs were on the opposite side looking out to the garden and the sea beyond. In the center was a long butcher's table with six chairs.

Directly from the table, three steps led to a square terrazzo patio surrounded by a low brick wall. Alongside the patio was a path lined with tiki torches called flambeaux.

After Julia set the table, she grabbed the matches and made her way down the path to light each flambeau. She stopped and looked up. A smile spread across her face as she stared at the moon hanging bright and glorious over Mount Arippo. It felt so near and more real somehow when she was on the island, her second home.

"Dinner is ready, RiRi." Her grandmother announced. Julia turned and walked up the path to sit beside her grandmother.

"So tell me how is school?" her grandmother broke off a piece of roti to use as a spoon to scoop up some of the eggplant mixture.

"School's good. I am doing good in English, so-so in science, okay in math and get this, pretty good in history. I seem to like ancient things." Julia said with a smirk.

"Watch it young lady, I am not ancient, just well-preserved," her grandmother retorted.

"No, seriously, I am intrigued by how things were in the past, that I really meant to say grams," Julia explained.

"Does that mean tonight you want one of those stories?" her grandmother played along.

"Yes, that would be great," Julia grinned.

Julia noticed how the conversation never turned to her summer plans or any mention of Jonathan.

After dinner, she did the dishes while her grandmother made tea. They returned to the veranda with their tea and cookies. They rested them on the small three-legged table between the rocking chairs, then settled in the chairs.

They sat contentedly watching the flickering flames of the flambeaux. Julia cast her grandmother a sidelong glance to see if she should mention story-time, the part of the evening she was looking forward to the most. Her grandmother was staring into the inky blackness towards the sea as if summoning memories from its depths than her imagination. Then without much introduction except for clearing her throat, her grandmother began.

"A long time ago, there was a tall man with a mustache and glasses who lived with his new bride, aged parents, two younger brothers and three sisters, with their husbands and children, on a large estate in India," Adhari said.

Julia carefully reached for her cup, blew into it, and gingerly took a sip as she settled in for the story. She loved the way her grandmother told stories in a slow, melodic voice. It gave her time to put herself in the story.

Her grandmother continued, "one day late in the afternoon, the local postman cycled up to the house as they sat around in the courtyard drinking *chai*. He pulled a thick, white envelope from his satchel and handed it to the tall man. The man thanked him and waited for the postman to leave before he turned his gaze to his father out of respect for him being the elder in the family. The man's father toggled his head from side to side to indicate that he could proceed. The man exchanged a quick look with his wife before he opened the envelope.

It was a letter from Mr. James, an owner of a sugar plantation in the West Indies, who needed the services of a plantation doctor. They would pay his passage or ticket for him and his wife if they agreed to a two-year contract."

"Wait, a two-year contract," Julia interrupted. "I actually learned something about this recently for a project I had to do at school on the history of indentureship."

"Yes, what did you learn?" Adhari asked.

"Well, the sugar plantations in the West Indies needed workers after slavery was abolished, so they hired workers from India. The women had three-year contracts and the men had five-year ones. Right?" Julia explained.

"Yes, that's right. What was different for papa Akash was that he lived in Jodhpur, Rajputana, which was not where the British Crown Agents recruited laborers from. Most came from other parts of India like Agra, Bengal, Delhi and the largest registrations came from Fyzabad. So to receive this personal invitation was special." Her grandmother affirmed.

"But why were so many people recruited? What was happening in India that made them leave?" Julia asked.

"That's a good question. Mainly poverty and high cost of grain.," her grandmother replied. "Now, it was the custom that before any big decision was made, it was first discussed with the whole family. After many evenings talking about the invitation, consulting a map to locate the West Indies and the fact that responsibilities will be shifted to other members of the family, they unanimously agreed that the man and his wife should go.

The man, whose name was Akash, wrote to Mr. James, the plantation owner, to let him know that he and his wife, Sushima, will be sailing in one month's time if all preparations can be made.

The journey was about three months long over rough seas. One afternoon, as the steamer made its way past the frigid winds off the Cape of Good Hope, Akash sat on the deck with face turned up to the sun. He had with him his writing box. He wanted to write home to his father. He knew he couldn't mail it until they docked but wanted to capture what it was like to be on a ship while he was on it," Adhari said.

"Wait grams, what is a writing box?" Julia asked.

"A writing box was a square or rectangular-shaped wooden box with either a flat or sloped lid used as a writing surface. It could store writing materials and important documents. It was sometimes lined with velvet or silk. It had deep pockets sewn against the interior panels with leather straps to hold upside down fountain pens. The outside was often inlaid with ivory, gold or polished wood and a decorative border," her grandmother explained.

"Okay back to the story," Julia said.

"He caught movement out of the corner of his eyes. A young girl of about twelve was crouched between two deck chairs with her face buried in her knees. She must have sensed someone looking at her because she looked up at him just in time. He smiled. She smiled back but it did not reach her sad eyes. There was something about the moment that made him hesitate to draw her into conversation. He was comfortable sharing the space with another person without being intrusive.

Although neither spoke, there was a small comfort from the presence and silence of the other, which, in an odd way, gave permission for each person to tuck back into themselves.

He returned to the familiar companionship of his thoughts. Staring out to the open sea, an expanse of unchanging blue above with a darker hue below, he turned inward. He soon noticed how his breath matched the rise and fall of the undulating ship. The sensation lulled his senses, and, in that moment, he wished for a hammock than a chair. Suddenly the girl spoke. She startled him and he gawked at her as though she had appeared out of thin air. He had forgotten all about her. He shook himself into alertness and asked her to repeat herself.

She asked him if he was planning to write home. He toggled his head from side to side giving his assent. Her eyes brimmed with tears. She begged him to write to her family. She explained how she had been tricked by her *mausi*, and *mausa*, aunt and uncle, who promised to take care of her and send her to school, but once they were on the ship, they told her she would have to work off her passage until they could arrange her marriage. She was scared and wanted to go home. He promised he would write to her family. But he knew how far away from home she would be, and it was unlikely her parents would be able to afford the ship's fare to sail there and get her.

In fact, many of the travelers aboard did not have the money for their ship's fare. They were given a work contract. When it ended, they could either stay no longer as an indentured worker or they could use their free return ticket home.

Days turned into weeks as they crossed the black sea. All there was to see was sky above and sea below. A month had passed when the travelers endured all manner of sickness at sea from respiratory problems to measles, but the worst kind was homesickness. By then Akash was known as the man with the writing box. The writing box had taken on an almost magical quality which carried safely in its deep inner pockets' letters filled with their longing for something better for themselves and their left-behind families.

Some knew their letters would never reach home because they couldn't afford the postage to mail it, nevertheless, they were comforted in the thought that their story, and their hopes were preserved. It was as though part of them would endure and perhaps be remembered. At times, the men would walk away feeling lighter whistling a village song after Akash wrote their letter," Adhari said. She saw the night air was getting cool and she was tired.

Julia stretched and yawned.

She was touched by this story, but also knew the trials and hardships they endured was not a singular experience. There was the abhorrent slave trade where princes and young men were taken from their tribes and kingdoms in Africa to face the horrors of the middle passage. She marveled at the strength of the human spirit to be strong despite adversity.

But she was ready to dock and more precisely find her bed. The wind had picked up and there was a chill in the air. She felt stiff sitting so long in the wooden rocking chair.

"Grams, I'm ready for bed," she said. She unfurled her legs from under her and stood.

Her grandmother slowly rose, "me too, *beti*," she said.

They slid open the sliding door, stepped into the living room and locked it behind them. They turned off the lights as they made their way to the bedroom hallway. It had a large single-pane window at one end. Bright moonlight shone through the window. They walked arm in arm down the shadowy hallway. Julia stopped when she got to her room. "Akash sounded like such a kind man. Who was he grams?" she asked.

"My grandfather," Adhari said, "Good-night my dear girl. Sweet dreams."

FIVE

———

THE NEXT THREE WEEKS, Julia, Jonathan and his sisters, Nalini and Shoba were inseparable. Either her grandmother, or Jonathan's mom, Kavita aunty would drive them either to the mall or to the movies. Sometimes Jonathan's school friends, Vijay, and Sheldon, met up with them for pizza. But her favorite part of her vacation was her grandmother's stories after dinner and recently her stories about what life was like during the colonial era when Indian labourers were recruited from India and brought to work on the sugarcane plantations. They were not indentured servants but were personally invited by Mr. James to work as professionals.

She was excited about tonight's story. Her grandmother promised to tell her how papa Akash and his wife left the plantation before their contract ended.

That evening, after dinner, Julia offered to wash the dishes while her grandmother made tea. They walked out to the veranda with their steaming cups of chai and settled in. Adhari chuckled and began.

"Where did we leave off?" Adhari asked.

"Papa Akash and his wife arrived in Trinidad." Julia replied.

"Right. They had sailed from the Port of Calcutta, India to the Port-of-Spain, Trinidad. He was a medic, and his wife was a midwife. When they arrived, they were given a small cottage on the plantation. They were expected to look after the staff and their families who either worked on the plantation or on the vast sugarcane fields. Their primary responsibilities were to bandage, birth or bury any worker or their family members who were under contract with the James plantation."

"Sounds like they had their hands full. No time to get homesick, I imagine," Julia remarked.

"Home. It came to take on a new meaning for them," Adhari said wistfully.

"What do you mean?" Julia asked.

"Once they were settled, they tasted something new – freedom from the caste system," Adhari said.

"Wait, I learned about this in history class," Julia interrupted. "The caste system in India was like segregation in America, but instead of two classes, black and white, in India it was four castes or classes of people."

"Yes. In fact, there were five castes you could say. There were the Untouchables, the outcasts. You see, a person is born into a particular caste. Their caste decides who they could marry, what kind of work they could do and basically where they belong in society, even what street they could walk on," Adhari explained.

"What street you could walk on?" Julia asked incredulously.

Adhari nodded. "But here on this island, it didn't matter what your caste was, or even what your religion was, they could now treat anyone who needed their help. There was just one condition. They could help anyone as long as they had a contract with the James Plantation. Most of the people they came into contact with, in one way or another, worked for the plantation."

"Tell me what papa Akash and his wife looked like and what was her name," pleaded Julia.

"Akash Tanwar was tall and handsome. He wore his hair and moustache trimmed and neat. He wore glasses and three-piece suits. It was said his head can usually be found in one of two places, either in the clouds or in a book. His wife, Sushima, was very beautiful. Her silky black hair cascaded down her back in soft waves. She lined her almond shaped eyes with black kohl. Two thin gold bracelets circled her ankles and tinkled when she walked bare-footed.

They had been there about a year. Then one day, mama Sushima went to the market to do the weekly shopping. Papa Akash was at home updating medical records. It was a hot day. The glaring sun shone bright white. There was a crush of people as Sushima made her way from vendor to vendor. Suddenly she heard a woman scream in pain and turned towards the sound. She scanned the crowd and spotted a young boy of about seven or eight running towards her. She dropped to her knees to be at his eye level.

"Are you the baby lady?" he asked panting.

"The baby lady, oh yes, I'm a midwife," she forced her voice to remain calm so as to calm him. He relaxed a little.

He grabbed her hand, "come miss please. It's me mudder. She havin' the baby now, she ballin' in pain. Hurry nah," he begged.

"Yes I'll help her. What is your name?" she replied letting him lead the way.

"Rishi," he said.

He took her to a row of shops with tin roofs alongside the west side of the market. She heard moans coming from a shop with cotton house-dresses swinging from the rafters. She walked into a dimly lit wooden shop that sold nighties, house-dresses, and stockings. The air was thick. Not even a slight breeze blew. She saw a woman lying on a cot in active labor and thought this must be Rishi's mother. Three women with anxious stares crowded around the woman on the cot.

She pulled out a handkerchief from her bag as she stooped down near the cot to wipe the pregnant lady's brow and introduce herself.

"I'm Sushima. I'm a midwife. I can help you. What is your name?" asked Sushima.

"Preeti. Thank you for coming," she said then sucked in her breath at the next wave of contractions.

The three women found their voices. The short, round one spoke first.

"I'm Babli. My shop is next to Preeti's. I sell sarees and lenghas for weddings," she announced pointing to her right.

"And I'm Angie, my shop is on the other side of Preeti's. I sell shoes and sandals," she said. She could be Babli's sister but with a more bronze look to her skin.

A tall slender woman named Sylvia said she owned the boutique and the bakery across the street.

"Ladies, I need your help. We need a basin

with hot water and clean towels. If I can have that quickly please. And a pair of scissors," Sushima said.

Sylvia looked at Babli, "come with me."

Now that Sushima got two of the women out of the way, she turned to Angie. "Angie and Rishi if you could go to the front and keep an eye on the shops, that would be good," Sushima said. She could now concentrate on Preeti.

Sylvia and Babli returned with the hot water and towels. Sushima asked Babli to find something to fan Preet with. She made Sylvia her assistant to help her with the delivery. Two hours later, she handed Preeti a pink healthy baby girl. She advised Preeti to still get checked out at the local clinic.

She left soon after with the promise to come check on her next week. She walked out of the shop exhausted but happy. She was now eager to get home and take a shower. Sweat trickled down her chest and back. But most of all, she was thirsty.

As she headed out the market, she saw Manny the coconut man and stopped to get a fresh cut coconut. Manny chopped off the top made a small hole and stuck a straw in it. She sipped on it as she walked back home feeling refreshed.

When she entered the yard, Akash was in front of their cottage with Mr. James, the estate owner, and Mr. Parker, the overseer. She figured she would say a quick hello and head inside. But as she approached, Mr. James addressed her.

"Mrs. Tanwar. I heard some interesting news today about your visit to the market," Mr. James announced getting straight to the point.

She looked over at Akash who wore a mischievous look on her face. She crinkled her brows. Mr. James stood foot planted with his hands clasped behind his back staring at her. Mr. Parker stood slightly behind Mr. James with a smirk in his face.

"What did you hear Mr. James?" she asked. Not taking the bait. For the most part, Mr. James was a fair and honest plantation owner. He was also a lawyer.

"I heard you helped someone at the market," he stated. He cleared his throat. "Allow me to rephrase that. Mrs. Tanwar, did you provide medical assistance today to someone who is not a contracted worker of the estate?"

Then it dawned on her why he was there. She gnawed on her bottom lip thinking how to respond. "I am trained as a midwife. Today, someone needed the help of a midwife, and I provided it," she replied.

"Mrs. Tanwar, your competence is not in question. You are highly competent," Mr. James said with a slight nod of acknowledgement. Then continued, "It is your compliance that is in question. By acting in the capacity as a midwife, you breached the terms of your contract which states you are only to provide services as a midwife to those contracted by the estate. The shopkeeper at the market is not under contract with the estate," he explained. He paused as though wrestling with himself for what he was about to say next. He turned to Akash. "Akash, I am left with no choice in the matter. I give you to the end of the month to vacate the premises. You are no longer employed by the estate. You are released from your contracts. This also means there will be no vouchers issued for return tickets to India. Should you wish to return, you will bear the costs." Mr. James put his hand out. Akash took it firmly in his, shook it and nodded. Then Mr. James left with Mr. Parker trailing behind him.

Sushima entered the cottage and dropped onto a nearby chair to take in all that had happened. Akash walked in and sat across from her. He took her hands in his to make her look at him. She lifted her eyes to his.

"You did the right thing helping that woman Sushima. I am proud of you," he said.

She smiled. "But now we have no home. Akash what are we going to do?" she asked.

"You're right we have no home. But we have three things," he paused, "and from where I sit, it's all we need. All we've ever needed," he declared cryptically.

"What are you talking about?" Sushima asked confused.

"First, we have means," he rubbed his fingers together. His voice low and steady, "second, we have dreams, and the best of the three, we have each other," he stated. He rose and spread his arms wide looking as regal as a king among his treasures. He motioned for her to come to him. She laughed and rose to go to him. She came close, but instead of walking into his embrace, she surprised him when she bent and touched his feet, a silent show of respect, then rose and folded herself into him.

One week later, they bought a two-story house. They turned the first floor into a clinic and made the second floor their living quarters.

"Grams what a beautiful story," said Julia yawning. "I wish one day I could have a love like theirs."

"I want that for you too, beta. The funny thing about life is sometimes, we're busy looking for the extraordinary, when what we need is right in front of us, just clothed in the ordinary," said Adhari.

They walked inside and turned off the lights. Julia went to bed that night thinking about how different life was during colonial times. Yet, in many ways, how we are all basically the same, wanting the same things like home, safety, family and love.

SIX

———

I

T WAS HER LAST WEEK of vacation. Her parents had arrived on Monday. On Friday they would meet up with the Sundars for oysters at Gary's Oyster Bar in Chaguanas, located in the center of the island. Then Saturday night dinner at the house with just the family and fly out early Sunday morning back to New York. That was the plan.

But that was still five days away, so she braced herself for the week ahead. Vacationing with her parents, specifically her father, was like being on holiday with a tourist and a local, an affliction he alone suffered from. He once said he learned about a place in two ways when he walked it and read about it.

Her father had already booked a guided tour to the bird sanctuary. And he would make a library run to stock up on books written by local authors for rainy days.

One year, Julia overheard her mother say to him, "Peter, you know you can buy books from local authors on Amazon from anywhere, right?" He had replied, "Yes that's true. But, if I can read a book by a writer while I am in their country, wouldn't it just make for a more authentic experience? It would be as though you can see what they saw sort of in the same way." Julia had never looked at it like that before but liked the idea.

Nevertheless, Julia knew two things that would never change were her parents' traditional values and their communication styles. Family time was important to them both. But they were completely different in how they communicated.

Her mother was quiet and contemplative. Her body in a restful pose with her head tilted to one side as she sat during unhurried pauses for Julia to reveal what was on her mind in the way she wanted to. Even when Julia would end her monologue with, "I don't think that came out the way I wanted it to," her mother would say, "then try again".

Julia had always felt a special bond with her mother and thought it may have to do with their nine-month cohabitation. From the outside, it looked as though theirs was a one-sided relationship since only one of them is on the outside. But that is not how she remembered it. To her, they did everything together. When her mother danced, or walked down the stairs, she did somersaults. When her mother napped, she did too, even if her naps lasted longer. And she ate and drank what her mother did. That's how she knew she didn't like peanut butter.

Her father, on the other hand, had an entirely different communication style. He entered each conversation like a traveler without a visa, so you never know when he would leave the conversation alone. He had a relaxed air about him like there was nothing else he would rather do at that moment than to sit and chat with you. He would sit with one leg over the other, his back nestled into the chair with arms lightly folded on his lap with his head cocked to one side.

It was both amusing and interesting to her how their body language had an influence on what Julia chose to share and how much. With her mother, she thought about how to phrase something. This always gave her a chuckle considering her father was the writer and wordsmith.

But when she talked to her father, she rambled. Her thoughts and feelings seem to bubble up and flow out her mouth. Yet with all this ease and openness, she clammed shut when it came to her feelings about Jonathan .

She didn't like to keep secrets from her parents. She thought secrets created barriers like low walls.

"Julia, are you outside honey?" Ana asked

"Yes mom," Julia answered. She was in the garden in the hammock that hung between two coconut trees. She planted her left palm on the grass to stop it from rocking and climbed out. She strolled towards the house where her mother waited for her in the shade of the veranda. As she neared, her mother said, "dad booked us a tour to the bird sanctuary to see the scarlet ibis. We leave in twenty minutes. Do you want to come?"

"Sure, I'll get dressed" Julia replied and walked inside.

"Don't forget your hat and sunscreen." Ana called after her.

"Got it, mom."

An hour later, they pulled into the bird sanctuary and were greeted by their guide, Thomas. Peter and Thomas helped Julia and Ana into the canoe, then climbed in and waded out into the murky waters of the mangrove. Julia had brought her camera along and hoped to get some great shots of the scarlet ibis in flight. When they turned the bend in the river, there they were clustered, in their regal scarlet-colored plumes. She held her breath as she stared at them mesmerized, then remembering her camera, she slowly raised it to her face. Her father did the same.

Suddenly as if by some silent signal, the birds

all seem to turn at the same time and look at them, then in one accord, took to the skies, a swath of red aloft.

The canoe slowly made its way back to the visitor's center. As they thanked the guide and drove home, Julia longed for a swim. She was hot and sweaty. There was a grassy lane like a footpath from her house to the beach.

"Mom, want to walk me down to the beach when we get back home?" Julia asked.

"Yes, that's a great idea." Ana replied.

They pulled into the driveway and Julia hopped out. "Mom, I'll meet you at the bottom of the garden. Be right out," she called out as she headed for her room to change. She wore an olive-green bikini under a pair of white shorts and a halter top.

Her mother waited for her at the bottom of the garden where the trace or footpath began. Julia was spraying her arms with sunscreen as she walked towards her.

When they got to the beach, Nalini and Shoba were sitting on a beach blanket eating sandwiches and watching a group of boys play cricket in the sand. Julia looked in the direction they were looking and recognized Jonathan, Vijay and Sheldon with some other boys playing a game of cricket. Jonathan's back was to her, but as she neared the beach, it was as though he sensed her arrival, turned and immediately their eyes met. He smiled a wide bright smile and waved to her, she reflexively did the same.

She turned to her mother, her pulse quickening, "Mom, Nalini and Shoba are here with Jonathan and his friends. So, I'll hang with them and see you back at the house later."

"Sounds good. Be careful," Ana cautioned and headed back up the path.

"Hey guys. Up for a swim with me after lunch?" Julia asked.

"Hey Julia! Sure. The water feels divine." Nalini said.

"Who is Jonathan playing cricket with? Are those his friends from school?" asked Julia looking in his direction.

"No, they're some random guys who were here when we got here." Shoba explained.

Then Julia heard her name. She looked towards the cricket game lacing her fingers to her eyebrows to shade her eyes from the sun's glare. She saw Jonathan waving at her to come join them. She shook her head and pointed towards the ocean. Then turned her head back to face Nalini and Shoba hoping they didn't see the flush in her cheeks.

She needed to do something with her hands, so she took of the baseball cap she wore, separated her thick hair into three parts and deftly started braiding her hair getting it ready for her swim.

It wasn't long before she saw Nalini and Shoba look past her shoulder to look up just past her. She turned and stared at a pair of long sapodilla-brown legs, as her eyes quickly shot up to see Jonathan towering over her.

As if on their own, her hands continued their practiced, rhythmic movements as she braided her hair. Jonathan watched her movements spellbound. He must have heard his sisters giggling because he cleared his throat pulling his gaze away to look out to sea at the sparkling turquoise bay as though he searched for a ship of courage to sail in. He combed his hair with slender fingers.

"Julia come play a game of cricket with me . . . I mean, us." Jonathan asked.

Another round of giggles came from his sisters. He glared at them. They quickly covered their mouths in a weak attempt to stifle them as he swung his gaze back to her.

"Me-I guess I could . . . I mean, um, you know I play soccer, right? I know how to play, but I don't really remember the rules of cricket," she said hedging.

"That's ok. I'll tell you what to do," his words stumbled out.

"Fine." She rose. They walked together to join the other guys who had stopped the game to wait for Jonathan.

"Hey guys!" Julia greeted them.

"Hiiiii Julia" they chorused. Jonathan rolled his eyes and shook his head trying not to look embarrassed. He walked up to Vijay, his best friend.

"Hey Vijay, Julia's playing. Pass her the bat," he said.

Vijay stared at his friend, then shrugged his shoulders and handed his bat to Julia.

"No, not that one. It's too heavy for her." Jonathan said. "The lightweight one."

This time Vijay had a smirk on his face when he handed the lighter weight bat to Julia. He knew Jonathan always had a thing for Julia but would never let her know.

Julia hefted it, getting a feel for it as she walked to the wicket. A gusty wind blew loosening strands of her hair from her braid. She stood at the base, feet apart and tilted her body a little forward. Her eyes fixed on Jonathan waiting for him to bowl as she rocked back and forth.

He scoffed the cock ball against his thigh a few times then broke out into a run towards her. Not her, but towards the wicket behind her.

In the game of cricket, the bowler starts off with a sprint to build momentum towards the wicket. His goal was to hit the wicket which was three vertical posts with a horizontal bar across it.

Julia saw Jonathan with the long sapodilla brown legs take off running towards her. His arms were raised as he prepared to fling the ball overhead at the wicket behind her. Adrenaline coursed through her body. She felt like she did when she played soccer. She inhaled deeply to steady herself and clear her mind.

She made quick mental calculations. The velocity of the ball flying through the air. The wind speed. The timing of the bat hitting the ball. The direction she would swing the bat.

She angled her body and raised the bat in readiness. *Twack!* she hit the ball and sent it sailing through the air. It went past the sand dunes, towards the parking lot. All eyes followed it.

Julia was supposed to make her runs but stood there. Immovable. Then she heard someone calling her name. It was Jonathan at the other end.

"Run Julia!" he yelled. His hands cupped around his mouth.

His voice jolted her. Alert now, she locked eyes with Vijay who stood poised and anxious at the other end with his bat.

Julia took off towards Vijay grinning wide. She felt exhilarated at making such a good shot. She could hear the guys, who were now all the way in the parking lot, screaming at each other to check under the cars to find the ball.

Then out of nowhere, Jonathan did the oddest thing. As Julia was midway up the pitch, Jonathan jogged up to Vijay, grabbed the bat from his hand to run towards Julia.

Julia could feel a trickle of sweat run down her spine. Jonathan ate up the sand between them with his long stride. She was near enough to search his face for an explanation for his odd behavior. His cheeks were red. She stopped. He did too. In the middle of the game, in the middle of the pitch, their closeness closing a door to the outside world of people. The only sounds to reach them were the crashing waves and their shaky breathing.

Julia felt herself spinning. With Jonathan's honey brown eyes searching her face, she felt her cheeks burn. She couldn't remember why she was there or what she needed to say or do. Her mind struggled to string words together to form sentences.

"You okay?" he whispered. A mix of curiosity and concern on his face.

All she could manage was a nod.

He laughed. Then brought his face near hers. So close she thought his lips would touch hers. She sucked in her breath. But his lips went, not to meet hers, but close to her ears. He purred with a low voice, "then Julia, run."

She found her legs and took off. She and Jonathan ran back and forth making their runs. After the sixth tap of the bat, she knew they won. Game over.

She dropped the bat. She pulled off her T-shirt as she ran to her beach towel. Yanked off her shorts, dropped it too on her towel and headed to the waves.

The foamy water rushed around her ankles. She saw a big wave readying to curl. She quickly skipped over the smaller ones to get closer. Right before it crashed, she dove under. Moments later, she surfaced and spread her arms wide as she floated on her back. She loved to swim in the ocean, and this one, Maracas Bay, was her favorite.

It was nestled between two mountains with a wide swath of white sand and tall coconut trees. She realized how attached she had become not just to the people on this island, but to the island itself. It had become her second home. But she couldn't linger too long in her thoughts, she had to head back home to get ready for the family dinner her grandmother made on the last evening of their trip. She swam to shore, grabbed her things and walked up the trace that led to the house

SEVEN

_____

T WAS THEIR LAST EVENING in Trinidad. An intimate family dinner at Ambar Taj. The sun made its silent descent off the horizon leaving behind streaks of pink, purple and orange in the sky. A cool evening breeze made the coconut trees sway.

Peter walked out to the veranda, took the three steps to the patio area and began to light the row of flambeaux tiki lights along the path, warning the whirring mosquitos to take their party elsewhere.

Adhari and Ana scurried around the kitchen to get things finished up as the evening sun threw shades of orange and pink on the walls of the kitchen while enchanting sounds of the sitar came through the radio from old Hindi film songs.

Julia stood in front of her closet deciding what to wear. She had come home from the beach, took a shower and had a nap. Now she was getting ready for dinner. She picked out a white cotton skirt that brushed against her ankles and a deep blue crop top. She slipped on gold hoop earrings, swiped a thin line of lip balm across her thin lips, reached down to hook a thin gold band around her ankles, twisted her foot from left to right as the caught a glint of the now burnt orange sun, feeling light and festive, did a twirl and headed out the door.

She walked into the kitchen to find her mother with floured hands standing over the kitchen table with six small beehive shaped lumps of dough filled with ghee, clarified butter lined up in a row, a floured board near her with one of the lumps of dough on it as she pressed and flattened it with her hands, then used a rolling pin to roll it out until it was a thin, flat disc shape. Her grandmother was by the stove manning a hot griddle called a *tawa*. She would lightly coat it with oil, drop the roti on it to cook, coat that with oil, flip it over to do the same on the other side before removing it.

Julia gave her grandmother a kiss and went to sit at the kitchen table to watch her mom roll out the dough. "You look lovely darling, I like those earrings," her mother cooed. "Thanks mom," she replied. She loved paratha rotis.

Just then, her grandmother heard one of her favorite old Hindi songs. A look crossed her face, her eyes became dreamy with a faraway look.

She sang, *"abhi na jaao chhod kar"* and looked at them.

Julia asked, "grams what does it mean?"

"I am not ready for you to leave", her grand-mother translated

Her grandmother continued, *"ke dil abhi bhara nahi"* but this time she translated right after, 'my heart is not satiated yet'.

Julia's thoughts turned inward. She marveled at how bittersweet this moment felt with three generations of women sharing space and time, she could almost feel this memory forming tracks in her mind to retrieve in some distant future.

The significance of the moment was not just the scene of them in the kitchen, but the feeling it had stirred within her. In some ways, this time together reached a part of her soul and nourished her, it comforted her. She was now sad to leave so soon. She also saw what a close bond her mother shared with her grandmother. She would see them do things in companionable silence together, but she thought it was her mother's way of making up for lost time when, in fact, it was that her mother enjoyed her time together. It was not out of guilt, but out of love.

Her grandmother's voice broke her out of her reverie. "Sorry grandma, what was that?" she asked.

"Dinner is almost ready. Can you set the table

in the veranda, light the candles and let your father know?" her grandmother repeated.

"Sure," Julia said leaving the table and walking to the cupboard to get dishes and glasses out.

When she walked out to the veranda, Peter was standing at the low gallery wall looking at the silvery sea.

"Hey dad, grams said dinner is almost ready," said Julia

"Great, I'm starved. What's for dinner?" he asked

"You'll see," Julia replied as she started to set the table. "I can't believe how much I will miss this place," she continued, "but I think I say that every year." She chuckled.

"I know what you mean. I feel like I'm in another world when I'm here. And there is something about this year that feels different, harder to leave somehow. This is why I look forward to these trips, it's like reuniting with an old friend," he said wistfully.

"Yeah that's how I feel too—reuniting—I like that word, it sort of implies we have a connection and we're picking up where we left off." She liked the idea of something that was established, not ending, but continuing, whether that applied to how she felt about the island, her grandmother or even Jonathan. She was happy her father used that word, reuniting, it was a word that matched how she felt.

She threw him a puzzled look and asked, "but you don't spend as much time here as I do, so how is it you could feel it as strongly as I do?"

He replied, "the encounters may be brief, but the impressions formed runs deep."

"Wow dad. Did you read that somewhere?"

"No, I didn't." As he went to the sliding doors to open it for Ana to bring in the trays. Ana followed by Adhari came outside bearing trays of food.

A cool ocean breeze stirred the frangipani flowers filling the air with their heady scent. Everyone settled around the table ready to enjoy a dinner best eaten by hand.

Julia scanned the table as her grandmother, seated at the head, scooped a little from each dish on the table onto her plate - curry goat, curried chickpea and potatoes, spicy mango chutney and roti. The only thing that was on the table just for her father was a small carafe of cold milk to take away the burning in his ears and tongue from the spicy food.

They ate under a beautiful, starry night sky. After dinner, they went to sit on the patio. As Peter stoked the fire pit, sending small sparks into the cool night air, Adhari asked him about his writing. He told her he's working with a new editor but offered nothing further. His gaze drifted upward and out toward the sea. Ana cocked her head to the side admiring the view.

Adhari took the hint and changed the subject. She turned to her daughter as she announced, "I checked on Kavita this afternoon. When I walked into the yard, Jonathan was sitting up on the mango tree looking lost." A jolt went through Julia. All her senses were alert at the sound of his name. She was careful to show no sign and so consciously tried to control her breathing.

She knew her grandmother and mother were about to talk about the baby and all the preparations for her arrival; so, she took a quick mental departure from the conversation and surroundings to imagine Jonathan sitting in the mango tree.

She had seen him sitting there before, his long legs dangling, swinging carefree looking out towards the cane fields. But her grandmother said he looked lost. Was he sad about her leaving, she wondered. She was about to explore this thought when she heard his name that evening for the second time.

"You know Jonathan wants to be a doctor someday, like you Ana," her grandmother casually announced, either unaware or deciding to ignore the delicacy of the subject.

She continued, "I know this is a decision between you and Peter, but we know the Sundars so well and they are a good family *nah*. And their boy, their only son, is doing so well, so ambitious, and good-looking. That's all." She folded her small papery thin hands, cocked her head to one side to offer Julia a small innocent smile.

Julia was alert to every movement her father made. She knew she was not allowed to date, much less mention marriage. All her senses were trained on him. She couldn't quite read his expression, but she knew the set of his jaw and the throbbing vein on his forehead meant he was working hard to hold his tongue. He rose to stand by the low wall. She was not afraid of his anger in the sense that he would lash out in rage. But the belt or a slap were not the only instruments of pain. Words can be too.

Her mother was still beside her. Tense. Then Peter and stared at Ana hard. Their eyes locked in private conversation. He drew away from the wall and took the seat beside her.

He sat on the edge of the chair like a cat ready to lurch. His large hands clasped in front of him, to anchor and steady him. His knuckles were white from the firmness of his grip. A shiver ran up Julia's spine at the uncertainty of what would happen next. A wave of sadness washed over her at the thought that there was no way she could talk to her parents about her feelings for Jonathan.

Ana understood that it fell on her shoulders to handle this delicate situation. She was caught in two worlds and two roles. Dutiful daughter and supportive wife. She might take her husband's side, it was biblical.

But, as so often happens, when back in the company of our childhood, we often return to ourselves as though unaltered. Or at least others expect us to have remained unaltered.

Going back to our childhood home can make it easy to also go back to our childhood selves. Perhaps it has to do with the familiarity of home habits, the patterns of how we speak to one another—with the same recurring conversations, and rhythms of daily life. It is only in adulthood one may wonder which side of me is my true self.

Then you realize not all the crevices of your cavernous heart can be filled just with the love of family. There is room, a need, for different kinds of love. The Greeks wrote of four kinds.

Ana turned towards her mother cautiously. Her gaze was not direct to provoke but for understanding. She breathed deeply and took her mother's paper-thin hands in hers and gently massaged it.

She asked in a low voice, "How's Kavita coming along?"

Ana had been to check on her two days ago and found nothing alarming. But wanted to change the conversation to a topic that was often discussed at home when she was growing up– medicine.

"She is prepared and in good spirits. Baby will come any day now. We do not expect any surprises, but you never know, even when it's not your first," Adhari replied.

"You know ma, when she comes home with baby, she will need her family's help," said Ana rising. She paused to look at her aging mother who still very much wanted to feel useful, and said, "and yours too." She caressed her cheek. Then walked up the steps to the veranda.

"Julia darling, can you help me take the dishes to the kitchen please?" Ana asked.

Julia bobbed her head up and down and followed her mother to the veranda.

They walked into the dark kitchen. Ana made her way to the double porcelain sink while Julia waited at the threshold for her mother to turn on the lights. She didn't want to take the chance to bump into anything with glasses in her hands. Her mother flicked on the lights and walked back to the sink to fill one side with hot soapy water. Julia placed the glasses in the water. She bent to open a drawer with dish towels when her father walked in.

"Where's mom?" Ana asked

"She said she was tired and wanted to get ready for bed." Peter said rolling up his sleeves in front of the sink.

Ana nodded as she filled the other side of the sink with water. Peter plunged his hands into the soapy water, pulled out a soapy hand and flicked a few drops at Ana. She squealed, giggling, she ran to the other side of the kitchen and turned on the radio.

Julia slipped out to find her grandmother.

She was brushing her hair in her room when Julia walked in.

"Did you have a good summer my dear?" she asked

"Yes grandma. I love it here. I will miss it and you so much," Julia said wistfully.

"I will miss you too, and not just me you know," Adhari said with a mischievous twinkle in her eye.

"Grandma!" Julia's eyes widened. She was shocked at her grandmother's implication that Jonathan might miss her too although she desperately wanted to know if he would.

"The house doesn't feel the same when everyone leaves, you know," Adhari sighed. "Anyway,

I will come in to say goodnight in a little while. I have something I want to give you."

"A present? But, why?" asked Julia puzzled

"It's something from the past," her grand-mother explained, "I'll make some tea and come," she said.

EIGHT

A LIGHT RAIN FELL. Julia wore a light robe over her cotton pajamas. She climbed onto the padded window seat under the misty bay window. She settled herself among the bank of pillows and reached for her phone that was on the little table next to the window seat. She wanted to shoot Samantha a quick text before it was too late, but then heard a knock at the door. She put the phone down and went to the door.

Her grandmother stood on the threshold; her hands wrapped around a wooden box. On top of the box was a bamboo tray with two cups of chai tea. Each cup of tea had a pair of coconut biscuits tucked into the corner of the saucer.

Julia took the tray with the tea things and set it on a small table near the window seat. She took a cup of tea and climbed back onto the window seat.

When her grandmother came to sit beside her, she noticed she didn't set the box between them, but she put it almost behind her. Julia thought it was strange since she guessed this might be her present. Why would her grandmother bring this box and then act like she did not want her to see it. Julia eyed her curiously above the rim of her teacup but decided to say nothing.

They sat in silence for a while. Adhari seemed to want to say something and was figuring out a way to say it.

Julia thought she would come out and ask.

"Grams, is everything okay? I know you're sad we're leaving. I am too. But I don't know, it just seems like you have something on your mind." Julia coaxed.

"Julia, you're young yet. But as you get a little older, you will face life's ups and downs. What I mean to say is, you might think your life is perfect and nothing would ever go wrong, but that's not how life works. No one is perfect; therefore, no one has a perfect life. You're going to face situations, at times difficult ones, and how you handle them can reveal parts of yourself you haven't met yet."

What on earth was her grandmother going on about, Julia wondered. She knew life was not perfect. But was it possible her grandmother knew about Julia's secret - that deep down, Julia felt that her little world was pretty close to perfect. Why would that change? How could it change?

"When things in life change, you could feel all mixed up. Confused. Happy, sad, even angry," her grandmother continued. You might even feel like you are unrecognizable to yourself. Like you're a different person."

"Sounds scary and a little weird. Okay, so what can I do?" Julia asked.

"Write," her grandmother replied.

"About what?"

"About how you feel. Write as angry Julia, or confused Julia, sad Julia or even scared Julia," her grandmother explained.

"Scared! What would make me feel scared?" Except for this conversation," asked Julia puzzled.

"Do you remember when my grandfather Akash kept the letters of the travelers on the passage from India?" Adhari asked.

Julia nodded.

"The travelers felt that the letters papa Akash wrote for them, and kept safe in his writing box, was in some small way as though a part of themselves were kept safe in that box," Adhari explained.

"A part of them? In what way?" Julia furrowed her brow. Julia only ever knew one part of her which seemed constant throughout her life. And in it there were the three people who were most important to her, her mother, father and grandmother. Only recently, Jonathan was slowly becoming the fourth person. Life for Julia was predictable. She had not experienced any real disappointment or loss to cause a shift in her perspective, her mood or personality. So she felt it hard to comprehend why would the travelers want to leave a part of themselves in a letter stored in a box.

"Well, they must have sensed or perhaps already experienced from being on the ship a shift in who they were becoming. One cause for that change could simply be that they found themselves in close contact with other castes. The overseers on the ship and in the plantation where they were headed were not sensitive to the strong feelings shared among the different castes. The letters of their journey, their sadness, their abiding love for them might one day reach their families who only had imprinted in their minds the version of their loved one when they lived among them. There was another reason too," her grandmother said.

"What was that?" Julia asked.

"Their feelings of hope, loss, and fear would somehow come through in their letters," Adhari said.

"How?" asked Julia

"By the words they chose. If the letters captured what they felt, I would imagine it gave them," she paused searching for the word, "permission to feel other emotions when they arrived in the strange new land without feeling disloyal to thoughts they once held as sacred. Julia, we are all made up of different facets to our personality. We shock ourselves, and others, when sometimes we seem to make decisions contrary to our nature and experience."

Adhari reached behind her and picked up the wooden writing box.

Julia gasped. Her hands flung to cover her mouth. Although she knew the story was true, she couldn't believe the real, tangible part of it was sitting in front of her to touch and hold.

"Is that what I think it is?" she asked incredulously.

Adhari nodded. "Yes, this is my grandpa Akash's writing box. And I want you to have it." She rested it on Julia's lap.

It was a heavy box. Julia stared at the striking image of a man wearing a turban with two long strands of pearls draped across on it on the hand-painted lid. She raised questioning eyes at her grandmother and lifted her brow. Her grandmother smiled through misty eyes but remained silent on the regal-looking man's identity.

Julia lifted the box to her face to get a closer look at each hand-painted panel. Painted on each panel were a pair of green parakeets perched on a neem tree. Then she lifted the lid to peer inside. It was lined all around with sapphire blue velvet. There were two silken deep pockets on one side and three leather straps to hold pens on the other side.

The past sat on her lap. She closed the lid of the box and passed her hand across it. She loved it but couldn't possibly understand why her grandmother would give it to her. Does her mother know of papa Akash's writing box she wondered.

"But why give it me grams? What will I do with it?" asked Julia

"Same thing papa Akash did. To write and to keep what you've written," Adhari stated.

"But to who?"

"Yourself—yourselves. The different versions of you as you face different things in life," said Adhari.

"But that's what I have my friends for, and mom and dad. I talk to them," Julia retorted.

"Do you tell them everything you think about?" Adhari asked. She fixed her gaze on Julia and whispered, "everyone you think about?"

Julia blushed.

"Sweetheart, I am not asking you to keep things from your parents. But a time may come when you may face a situation, and if you're anything like me, you keep it to yourself until you know your mind on the matter before talking about it to others. It's those times you can write about it. Put it in the box. Go about your life and come back to it later. The time away from your written thoughts creates a little distance. That distance is called perspective. The time away also reveals if you still feel the same way. You might ask yourself what changed and why. That process is called insight." Adhari concluded.

"So, the writing box can help me gain perspective and insight?" Julia asked.

"The process can," Adhari replied.

Julia felt this was the most adult conversation she had ever had with her grandmother. She looked at her with new eyes. Her grandmother, a woman of stories, mystery and secrets. Adhari then reached over and picked up the box. She lifted the lid and slid her hands into one of the pockets and drew out a small leather purse. It had a key inside.

"This is the key to the lock," she said handing it to Julia and rested the box on the window seat between them.

"Oh. Thanks. This has been the most unusual night, I have to say. I was not expecting this gift," Julia declared.

"There is one more thing before I say good-night. I want you to know Julia no matter what happens in life, seasons of change may come, you Julia are the only one . . .”

Suddenly the door was wrenched open. Ana walked in breathless. “Mom, come quick! Come now, it’s Kavita. Baby’s coming!” Ana panted as though she had been running a mile to the house instead of just coming down the hallway.

Adhari quickly rose to her feet, “where’s Sundar?”

“At work. Can’t reach him, maybe no signal,” Ana gushed. “She needs you. Do you want Peter to drive you?”

“No, I’m not sure how long I’ll be gone,” Adhari replied.

She followed Ana out the room, then stopped and turned to Julia who was close behind, “I’ll tell you the rest tomorrow. Get some sleep. You fly out in the morning.”

Julia bobbed her head up and down. Gave her grandmother a quick hug and closed the door to her room. She yawned. Her back felt stiff. She stretched and headed for bed knowing it would be late before her grandmother returned.

NINE

———

THERE WAS A HUSHED SILENCE in the house as Julia slept. It felt pensive as an inhaled breath. Not every bed had dented pillows, warm bodies and sweet dreams. In the living room, Peter and Ana sat in the dark with the light from the hazy moon seeping in. They had not slept all night. They waited for Adhari to come home from the hospital which was forty-five minutes away.

Adhari had called from the hospital to say that Kavita had the baby and they were both doing fine and sleeping. Mr. Sundar, who worked the night shift at the wastewater sewer facility, had left work and was now there with them so she was leaving the hospital and on her way home. That was two hours ago.

"Peter I'm worried," said Ana. She rose and walked to the foyer to look out the back window.

Her eyes strained to see through the foggy weather for headlights coming up the driveway. Peter saw how worried she was. He was worried too.

"I'm getting worried too Ana," he said. He pushed himself off the sofa and walked to the foyer next to Ana. He sat on the bench against the wall. It had outside shoes under it. He pulled on a pair of boots and reached for the parker hanging on a hook above it. He jammed a baseball cap on his head and gave Ana a hug. "I'm going to find her," he declared.

She smiled with a mixture of relief and gratitude. "Thank you. Be careful out there, the roads are slick and wet." He went out the door. Got in the car and backed out the driveway.

Some hours later Julia stirred. The smell of brewing coffee made her think she was already back in New York. She unfurled from the fetal position, stretched and gently knuckled at her sleepy eyes. She peeked through the mosquito net and realized she was still in Trinidad. She panicked. Did they miss their flight? She knew she had to be up early to get ready, but judging from how light it was outside, it felt more like 8AM. Their flight was at 9AM. She flung the covers to one side and headed for the bathroom. She wondered why the house was so quiet.

She hurried to brush her teeth, wash her face and get dressed. She dropped the towel on her bed and headed out the door to the kitchen. Her mother was pouring two cups of coffee when Julia walked in. She looked up at her with red-rimmed eyes, a look of shock and alarm crossed her face. She quickly looked at Peter who was sitting at the kitchen table with the *Guardian* newspaper opened in front of him.

"What's wrong?" Julia asked. She caught the silent look that her parents exchanged with one another. She knew that look. It meant something happened and they were deciding who would be the one to tell her and how much they would say. She saw it when she came home from school one day and couldn't find Toby, her dog. She knew he was old and sick. They had that same look. They couldn't meet her eyes for a while. Then she looked around. Someone was missing.

"Where's grams? Didn't she come home from the hospital?" Julia asked, getting worried now. Ana came and pulled her into her arms. *Okay this is not good if mom is trying to comfort me.*

Her father pulled out a chair next to him and patted it. She walked over and took it.

He leaned forward to look her in the eye. "Julia, do you remember that we got the call last night for your grandmother to go over to help Mrs. Sundar with the baby?" All she could manage as tears welled up in her eyes was to bob her head up and down. The mind leaps to conclusions long before words offer a full explanation, so each time Peter paused to collect his thoughts, Julia's mind raced ahead to imagine the worst. While the reverse seems to happen when you hear the worst.

"Your grandmother," continued Peter, "did help Mrs. Sundar. She took her to the hospital. She had the baby and they're both doing well." After a long pause, he continued, "but" he looked at Ana, then shifted his eyes back to hers, "on the way home your grandmother had an accident."

Julia felt like something exploded in her head. She seemed to have trouble taking normal breaths. "Wait, what!" she asked. Then not waiting for another properly phrased answer, "is she okay? Where is she? Why isn't she home yet? What happened? Wait, did she even come home last night? Oh my god!" Julia pushed the chair back and stood up. She needed to be upright. Ready to go—somewhere. Her mother came and stood by her. She did not want to crowd her, so she didn't hold her but she saw how agitated she was.

"She was on her way home." Her father said in a steadying voice which somehow made the panic well up in her ebb. She stopped pacing but still wired, stood with her back against the kitchen counter.

Peter continued, "the roads were wet. She was not far from home. There was a truck coming around the bend. She didn't see it in time to swerve. They collided. Her car slid into a ditch," he paused.

Unchecked tears streamed down Julia's cheeks. Her lips trembled. "How—how, how long was she in the . . ." she swallowed, she couldn't bring herself to say ditch, "for dad?"

"An hour or two."

"Your dad found her," Ana said, a voice a faint whisper.

"Yes," Peter affirmed, "I took her back to the hospital where she had just come from. They are running tests. I waited for her to get a room. She has one now. She's resting. She'll be okay. We can see her after you've had something to eat." He was finished. It was all she was going to get from her father, the wordsmith.

She turned to her mother. She needed to know a little more. Perhaps she needed to prepare herself for what she was about to face going to the hospital. Her mind reeled with questions. How long was her grandmother in the ditch, cold and alone before her father found her? Did the truck total her car? Did she have a lot of bruises? Her grandmother was a small woman. Was anything broken? Would she need rehab or surgery? She lived alone. Who would take care of her while she recuperated? "Mom, was she conscious?" Julia asked.

Her mother looked up as though trying to decide how much to let on. "Barely," she uttered.

"Dad how did you know she was lying there?" Julia asked.

"When I went looking for her, I saw skid marks on the road to the house and saw some that lead there. We found her in time Julia. Let's have a little breakfast and then head over to see her, what do you think?"

"I'm not hungry, can we go now?" She pleaded with her father.

"We can, but it's seven in the morning and visiting hours is not for another two hours. Your mom was about to make some tea and toast." Julia nodded and sat back down.

TEN

———

W HEN THEY GOT HOME from the hospital, Julia went straight to her room. She wanted to be alone. She sat on the bed and pulled out her phone to text Jonathan to congratulate him on the baby, then decided against it. She spotted the writing box on the table. She picked it up and brought it back to her bed. She opened the lid, took out a sheet of paper and laid on the closed lid. She pulled open her nightstand draw for a pen.

Dear Writing Box, I don't know how this is going to help but I'm worried about my grandmother. If I tell mom and dad, they'll just tell me not to worry. But how am I supposed to not worry. Worrying is not just for adults. My grandmother was always so capable and independent. I never saw her sick. When I walked in and saw her lying in that hospital bed, I was scared. I don't want my grandma to die. When she opened her eyes and looked at me, I know stroke or not, that was still my grandma. On the way home mom and dad talked about having a day nurse come in to help grams when she comes home from the hospital. How can a stranger take care of my grandmother while we live so far away? She might feel we abandoned her. I can't do that. I want to stay here and help take care of her. I know my parents, especially my father, would say it's out of the question. I need courage. I know this is the right thing for me to do.

Julia folded the letter and tucked it inside a deep pocket in the writing box. She needed a nap.

She woke up when the sun cast a purplish orange glow in the sky. She walked out to the garden to her favorite shady spot which had a hammock, and a set of wrought-iron table and chairs. From this spot, she could see the winding road down below. She got in the hammock and rocked slowly.

She saw her mother coming up the path carrying a tray with two glasses of lemonade.

"Hey honey, I thought I might find you out here. Want one?" asked Ana

"Sure. Thanks mom," Julia said reaching for the glass.

There was a small blue wrought iron table with two chairs. Her mother laid the tray on the table and took a seat.

"Mom is grandma going to be okay, like really?" Julia asked.

"Oh honey, I can see how worried you are. But I'll be straight with you. The stroke left grams with some paralysis. She will have slurred speech and will tire easily. We asked Mrs. Scott to come help when she comes home from the hospital," Ana said.

Julia was quiet as she absently tugged at her ear. "Mom, I would like to stay back to help grams."

"Sweetheart, that is very thoughtful of you. But your father and I can't allow that. I know you are concerned about your grandmother, but we hired someone with medical experience and you have school. Here's what I can do. Instead of waiting until next summer, we will come back during the winter break so we will see her soon. What do you think?" Ana asked. Julia nodded.

"Mom when do we leave for New York?"

"Tomorrow morning," Ana replied.

The next morning, they flew back to New York. School was starting in a little under two weeks. Between back-to-school shopping, catching up with

Samantha and soccer practice starting, Julia had little time to check-in with Jonathan.

Then right after the Labor Day weekend, Julia looked out her window to see a yellow school bus coming up her street. She grabbed her backpack and hurried down the stairs. Her father was in the kitchen. She rushed in grabbed her water bottle and a bag of chips for the ride back home and headed out the door.

"Hey dad," Julia said. Peter was having a cup of coffee at the kitchen table.

"Good morning honey. First day of school. Time for a picture?" Peter asked holding up his phone.

"Dad, please no. I'll miss my bus," Julia said and rushed out the door.

Sundays was the one day when they were all home together. Ana sometimes had to work a double at the hospital, but Sundays were sacred. Not sacred in the sense that they observed the Sabbath or went to church, but in the sense, it was family time. Julia had just finished writing a paper for her English lit class and needed a break.

She walked into the living room. Her parents were on the sofa, so she plopped down on the rug. Her mother laid on the coach reading a medical journal her legs outstretched. At the other end, her father sat with a leather journal on his lap making notes.

She realized she needed something to rest her head on. She sprang up, yanked a pillow from behind her father and laughed at her stealth. She dropped back on the rug and tucked the pillow under her head.

"Hey, I was using that," he laughed, and leaned over to Ana pretending to see what she was reading and slipped the pillow from under her head with a triumphant cheshire cat grin. "Hey!" she growled at him and laughed.

After Julia settled back on the rug, her thoughts turned to her grandmother. "Mom, any news on grandma?" Julia asked

"Nothing new. She's home from the hospital. Mrs. Scott comes every day to check on her, fix her something to eat, water the plants, that kind of thing. I did speak to her physical therapist and grandma is cooperating. So that's good," Ana reported.

"Are we still planning on seeing her during the winter break?" asked Julia

Her mother hesitated, then said, "Yes". Julia caught it and wondered why her mother sounded uncertain.

"Dad are you coming too?" Julia asked. She

sensed something was going on and she wasn't sure if it had to do with her grandmother, her mother's work schedule or something else.

Peter cleared his throat and shot a look at Ana. "We'll see pumpkin," he said. Julia dropped it. She figured she will get the scoop from Jonathan if it has to do with her grandmother.

After a while, her mother closed the journal and got up to start dinner. She looked at Julia, "want to help me honey?"

"Sure mom," Julia got up off the rug with the throw pillow in her hand. She walked past Peter then abruptly pivoted on her heels to toss the pillow at him. It hit his shoulders. He feigned hurt. "Ah! At least you remember to return what you stole," he yelled. She laughed and headed to the kitchen.

The autumn air was thin and crisp. Julia enjoyed this time with her mother. Ana prepared the chicken and slid it in the oven. Julia set the pot of water on the stove to steam the asparagus. They talked about the upcoming Fall Fair at school. Her mother volunteered each year.

"By the way, I'm getting ready to email the link to the parents so they can select their time slots to volunteer at the Fall Fair. Did you have a preference where you want me this year? Inside or outside?" Ana asked.

"Didn't you sign up for the games outside last year but then also ended up having to help out inside with the candle making too?" Julai pointed out. Ana nodded.

"Okay, so which do you prefer mom, inside or outside?" asked Julia

"I don't have a preference. I just love being there. Maybe I'll wait to see if there are any vacant spots and I'll just fill in as needed," Ana said. "You know, I was at the store picking up some more prizes the other day and ran into Mrs. Grotter."

Julia looked up shocked. "You did?" she asked incredulous. Since she came back from Trinidad, Samantha did not once ask about her vacation. That was not like her. Julia knew Samantha was a camp counselor that summer. She did not think to invite her to Trinidad again this summer. But if she was honest with herself, was it because she knew she was working this summer or was there another reason? She didn't want to explore it. She just knew she was happy for her and had asked her about it.

"Did something happen between you two?" her mother asked.

"I don't think so. But still, I get the sense that something is up with her. I don't know what to do, mom." Julia said confused.

"When was the last time you saw her?" Ana asked

"At soccer practice on Friday."

"How did she seem to you?" Ana wanted to validate Julia's concerns but also didn't think there was anything to worry about.

"I don't know just a little distant. Less chatty. Less," Julia searched for the right word, "sharing. I felt like before I knew what she was up to, now when I reach out, she leaves me on read, she sometimes will text back with 'not a good time' or 'I'm busy, talk to you later."

"I have an idea. We need to go to the mall to get you some sweaters for school, ask her if she wants to come," Ana suggested.

"Good idea. I'll ask her," Julia said excitedly.

"Great. Now go find your father and tell him dinner is ready." Ana chuckled. She opened the oven door to check on the roast.

Julia found her father in the writing shed at the back of the house. She poked her head in. "Mom said dinner's ready."

"Great. I'm starved." Peter rose. They walked back inside together.

ELEVEN

O LD MAN WINTER CAME ambling along
bringing a light dusting of snow one
evening. Julia hopped off the school
bus which dropped her off by the big oak tree on
the corner of her street. She walked up the driveway and opened the back door to the kitchen. Her
mother was in the kitchen with a wooden spoon
stirring chili in a large stockpot.

"Hi mom. Smells good. When's dinner?" Julia
asked. She dropped on the nearby bench and pulled
off her short boots.

"As soon as your father gets home," Ana replied. "How was your day honey?"

"Good," said Julia. Heading for the stairs. "I'll
be right back." When Julia walked in her room
and dropped her backpack on the floor next to her
desk, her phone dinged. It was Jonathan. A smile
broke out on her face.

"Hey stranger! What's up?" Jonathan texted.

"Hey u. Not much. And u?" she tapped with a smile emoji.

"Nothing much. Btw, I checked on your grandma the other day. We sat and talked . . . about u."

"Me?! Wait . . . grams spoke?" A rush of excitement and worry ran through her.

"Well, not exactly. I could just tell she misses you. Lots of people do. Anyway, do you guys think you will be back here again this year? Or not till next summer?" Jonathan asked.

Julia heard the car door close. She knew her father was home. Then a few moments later, she heard her mother yell 'dinner's ready. Dad's home.'

"Mom said something about coming for Xmas. But nothing for sure yet. Hey, I gotta go. Talk later?" she tapped the message, then dropped her phone on the bed not waiting for a reply and headed downstairs.

Her mother filled three deep bowls of chili and put them on the counter to cool. She looked up when Julia entered the kitchen, "hey honey, can you set the table please?" she asked.

"Sure mom," said Julia

She walked to the adjoining room, slid open the pocket doors that led to the dining room. Her father had walked in and was washing his hands in the kitchen sink. He then took out a roll of sourdough bread to slice.

They sat down to dinner and talked about nothing and everything. Her grandmother's health, school and soccer.

"Hey dad, how's it working with a woman editor? You've never had to work with a woman before." Julia asked. She didn't see her mother's back stiffen and how fixed her eyes were on the bowl of chili in front of her.

Peter coughed to stall. "It's . . . am . . . it's a new experience, by the way anything we need to discuss before the next parent-teacher conference? Will there be any surprises?"

"No, so far so good. I'm not sure about math. You know how I struggle," Julia sighed.

"Do you think a math tutor would help? I could set that up for you if you'd like?" Ana said. She tried to read Julia's face to determine if Julia was being serious or modest. Julia laughed and rose to take her dishes to the kitchen.

"I didn't fail the first math test, so let's see how I do for the mid-term before we decide," she negotiated.

After dinner Julia went up to her room to get homework done.

Later that evening she decided to come

downstairs for a snack. The dimmer lights were low in the kitchen, but a light came from the living room. She walked in to find her mother sitting on the sofa. Hunched over. Eyes and nose rimmed with red. A large tissue box beside her thigh. Her father sat at the other end as though he heard bad news, a six-mile stare fixed on the zebra-striped carpet. He didn't look up when she walked in.

Julia's heart beat a tattoo against her chest. "What is it? Is it grams?" she demanded as she took short gulps of air preparing her mind for the worst.

"Julia have a seat. Since you're here we could as well tell you," Peter said his voice low and steady.

Julia sat on the ottoman facing them both.

"You know your mother and I love you very much," Peter began. He hunched forward and held his hands clasped in front of him to steady him. Julia stared at him hard, her brows furrowed of their own. There was silence. She couldn't stand it. She broke it, "what's going on that you're not letting me know. I'm not a kid. What is it?" She could see there was an inner struggle her father was wrestling with. He took a deep breath, cleared his throat, shot Ana a look and said, "your mom and I are getting divorced." He let the deafening silence roar. Then more resolute, he reassured, "but nothing will change when it comes to you. I will be at your games just like before. I will see you on the weekends . . ." then his voice trailed off careful to not make promises to replace guilt.

Julia felt her head about to explode. The spacious room felt like a cell. She needed air. She looked at her mother's face to see if what she saw there could confirm or deny what she just heard. Her mother's eyes held the deepest sadness she had ever seen before, and she knew it was true. Suddenly, anger took hold of her. Her secret. Her identity. The truth she told herself and only to herself that her life was perfect because the two people responsible for her creation made it so was no longer true. It was not perfect. It had just become pure hell. And the two of them just sat there—calmly, like they're having Sunday tea.

Julia couldn't sit there still and quiet like them. She sprang from the ottoman ready to leave. Then she stopped midway to address her father. "Why is this happening? I thought we were happy?" she demanded an explanation.

"I do not want to hurt you. Nor your mother. But we're not," her mother shot him a look that said don't you dare speak for me, you've lost the right to—he corrected, "I'm not happy. I fell in love with someone. Maggie," he stopped speaking abruptly. But Julia caught how he said Maggie with affection, savoring the name on his lips as though he was saying it to himself.

"Maggie! Your editor!" Julia shouted, purposely saying her name with derision. He looked at her sharply. His jaw set.

"Julia, your mom and I will always be your parents. We both will be actively involved in your life," Peter said. Falling back into the old marital ways of speaking for the both of them.

"Great! How nice and tidy. FOR YOU but absolute disaster FOR ME! You can go back to your former selves before you met each other. Or maybe for dad the new version of him with this Maggie," she spat out. "But what happens to me? I am here because of the union of you too. Ugh! When that is no more, what becomes of ME? Huh? My life was perfect." She didn't even care anymore if her secret was out. It was their fault it was created in the first place.

And equally their fault it was now destroyed. Forever. Nothing will ever be the same again. Ever. Her mother's sadness vanished; replaced by a look of distress. She was worried about her daughter's reaction to the news. She herself had never experienced anything like it before and felt ill-equipped to help.

"How could you guys just sit there so—calmly," she was sobbing now, her words coming out between hiccups. "I can't be here anymore." She got to her feet and ran to her room taking the stairs two at a time.

She imagined they had months to talk about and come to terms with it. She was not given that luxury. She now had to bear the weight of it like a living breathing thing beside her. She entered her room and crumbled to the floor, her chest heaving, palms clammy. She rocked on her heels back and forth, a low moan coming from deep within her like a wounded animal.

There was a light tap on the door and then it opened. Her mother came to join her on the carpet. She wrapped her arms around her shoulders and said softly, "I booked us two tickets to see your grandmother. We leave tomorrow." All Julia could manage to do was bob her head up and down. They hugged each other, each finding comfort and steadiness to ride the wave of turmoil.

TWELVE

T HE PLANE LANDED in the aftermath of a monsoon rain. Steam billowed up from the hot asphalt making the air foggy. The airport crew holding large black umbrellas ushered the passengers from the runway to the cavernous solemn building like a funeral procession.

Once inside, Julia and Ana whisked through customs. Mr. Patrick was not on duty, but Mr. Kevins were, and he made quick work of it. Julia and Ana had just their backpacks and no checked bags to wait for. They quickly joined the throng exiting the airport and found Mr. Sundar waiting for them at the terminal. He spotted them first and waved.

As the car climbed the mountain to Ambar Taj, Ana asked about Kavita and the kids. Julia enjoyed hearing about all the little things baby Joy was doing but when the conversation turned to the coming elections in the country, she knew there would be no news about Jonathan so she tuned out and stared out the window. Then she heard his name. She wondered if she was dreaming.

"I remember those days," Ana said.

"Yes, he's hitting the books hard. He's up all hours of the night studying for exams. If Jonathan is not at school or home, he's in the library. I hardly see him going out to lime or hangout with the fellas. His mother fusses at him that he's not getting enough rest." Mr. Sundar said with a touch of pride.

Julia felt like a stone was in the pit of her stomach. She had hoped to see him, even for a little while. They were only there for the weekend. But it sounded like he wouldn't come to see her with exams coming up. She knew how serious he was about school.

Mrs. Scott was waiting for them when they pulled up the drive. She smiled wide when she saw them. She was glad Mrs. Scott, a retired nurse and old friend of her grandmother, had been there daily to check on her grandmother. She wished there was something they could do to thank her.

Ana came out of the car. She crossed the threshold, shrugged off her backpack and hugged Mrs. Scott. Mrs. Scott's eyes brimmed with tears as she hugged her back.

"You can't imagine how thankful we are to have you here to check on mom Mrs. Scott, words can't describe my gratitude" Ana gushed. Mrs. Scott's cheeks reddened. "I brought you a little something from New York," Ana said and turned to open her backpack. She pulled out a wrapped parcel and handed it to her.

Mrs. Scott opened it and saw a beautiful silk scarf the colors of a peacock. She held it to her chest and closed her eyes. Then hugged Ana again to thank her.

Her mother's thoughtfulness and gratitude for what Mrs. Scott did for the family, considering all the recent developments, impressed Julia and taught her that it was still important to think of and to acknowledge the kind acts of others. To not be so absorbed with our own problems to miss these opportunities to show gratitude.

As they walked down the hallway to her grandmother's bedroom, Julia trailed quietly behind. She stole a glance at her mother and saw such serenity in her eyes.

When they entered, Adhari Perla was sitting propped up by a bank of pillows. She wore a long cotton nightgown. She offered a weak smile which caused her left lip to droop. Julia thought she looked like a little bird in a big nest. She slid in the bed to snuggle with her. She rested her head in the crook of her bony neck.

"Hi grams. Missed you lots," Julia said. Adhari patted her hair and Julia bent her head low so her grandmother could kiss her forehead. It seemed that in the short time she was away, she had shot up another couple of inches.

"Hi mom. You look good," Ana said. Her smile soft and gentle as she took her mother's frail hand in her capable ones.

The room fell silent as each person struggled in that moment in their own private way to face the alterations Adhari had undergone. She needed total assistance for every aspect of daily life, from bathing to dressing to fixing meals and eating them. Her face drooped on one side and on the same side her arm had little strength.

Although Ana was more at home in the doctor-patient mode, she had no prior knowledge in the "mother as patient setting." Her role and her understanding required her to understand how to dispense medical care with a new brand of compassion. It was a lesson that would come to change the way she interacted with her patients and their families in the future. When illness touches you at home, the world can come to feel smaller, more like a community. Another person's mother, or sister or brother who is sick, it's like your own is sick.

"Talk to her. She can hear you," Mrs. Scott's soothing voice suggested. Startled at the sound of her voice, Ana and Julia swiveled their heads to stare at her having forgotten she was there.

Ana nodded. She scanned the nightstand. She saw a jar of cocoa butter. She walked over, scooped it up and perched on Adhari's bed. She began massaging the butter into her hands, then hitting her stride, she decided on her legs next. She felt her mother's body relax and loosen as though she had been carrying the weight of her entire condition all alone.

The weight of the unwell is not always a condition of the body, that can be measured in pounds. But how does one measure emotional weight, a weight that rests in the mind? Where does one feel the heaviness, the load? Is it carried on the shoulders? The neck? The temples? The evidence is not in the seeing eye but the discerning mind. There are signs. If you know where to look.

But where are the signs? The deep grooves between the brows perhaps? Shallow breaths? Smiles like a nomad's trek through the desert seeking refreshment and vitality? Or lackluster eyes?

Julia was lulled by the atmosphere of togetherness and of care. She curled up next to her grandmother and soon fell asleep. She woke up a little while later as the evening drew near, powerfully hungry. She had skipped lunch. Her grandmother snored softly beside her. Her mother walked in and motioned her to meet her outside.

"Your grandmother already had dinner and her medication. She will sleep through the night. Why don't we get you some dinner. Kavita sent some food over. I'll heat it up for you. Julia nodded. She told her mother she needed to shower, change into pajamas and will be right back.

Julia walked into her room and opened the windows to feel the ocean breeze. She hoped she and her mother could sit in the veranda for a little while tonight to look up at the moon. Although she had been with her mother the whole day, she felt she needed this time with her alone; possibly as a way to process the day with someone instead of apart. She showered, changed into a pair of cotton pajamas, but walked with a sweatshirt just in case.

Ana had two bowls of steaming fish broth soup with thin dumplings. It was exactly what she wanted, something light but tasty and filling.

"Where are we eating mom?" Julia asked. Grabbing a potholder to place hers on a plate. She rested a spoon next to it.

"Outside," said Ana. Doing the same with her plate.

"Where's Mrs. Scott? Is she going to join us?" asked Julia. Peering into the living room.

"She went home. Since we're here, she doesn't have to spend the nights." Ana explained.

"So just us?" Julia stated more than asked. Smiling.

"Yes. Is that alright? I was hoping we could have some time together. I want to know how you're doing?" Ana said. She wouldn't normally welcome her mother reading her mind, but Julia was happy they were on the same page.

"No, I'm glad it's just us. Well, it would have been better if dad was also here . . . oh . . . I'm . . . I'm sorry . . . um . ." Julia stammered and looked away.

Ana eyes welled up and she swatted the tears away. She stood up and walked to the low wall on the patio. Collected herself and came back up. "It's okay darling. We both have to find a way to make adjustments to the news and our new circumstances. I know we haven't had much chance to talk openly about all that you're going through dealing with this. So I'm here for you. This is not just a trip about your grandmother, it's also about you. So anything you want to talk about or ask. I may not always be up to talking about it for a long time, but I will try to always be here if you want to talk. Deal?" All Julia could manage as the tears rolled down her cheeks was to nod and reach for her mother's embrace.

They ate outside with a bright crescent moon high in the sky. Julia can't remember a time when she felt closer, and in some way, more protective of her mother than sitting with her here tonight. After dinner, they did the dishes and turned it down on the drainer to dry. They made two cups of chai and returned to their spots to sit and chat.

"Mom, can I ask you something?" Julia asked shyly.

"Sure honey," Ana blew on her tea to cool it before gingerly sipping it.

"Why don't you tell dad you don't want one?" Julia stated flatly.

"Don't want one of what?" Ana caught her eyes and furrowed her brow.

"A divorce. You and dad. Why are you letting him just walk away. Why don't you fight for him?" Julia explained.

Tears, with their quick and easy appearances these days, sprang up in Ana's eyes. Her lips quivered as she was about to speak. She placed trembling fingers over them to still them and looked away.

Julia saw the immense hurt her thoughtless question caused and wished she had remained quiet or that she knew how to ask it another way. She sat quietly. She decided not to say anything else that could hurt her mother. She would wait until she was ready to speak, even if it meant her mother may not answer her burning question.

Her mother rose and walked inside. Julia felt a pang of hurt and rejection. Her mother said not one word. She just left her sitting there. Was it so bad to want to ask why these two people made such a major decision about their lives—her life—and she can't get an explanation. She was not a child.

Then her mother walked back in with a book in her hand.

"I'm sorry I walked away. I wanted you to read this, it might help makes some sense for you. It was the only thing that made sense to me." Ana said and handed her a book of poems by Catallus. "If you wouldn't mind, can you read it alone. I will be in my room if you want to talk later. If not, good night my darling. And know that I speak for both your dad and I, we love you for miles and miles. That will never change." She kissed her forehead and rose to walk back inside. She stopped, "the eighth poem."

Julia decided to go to her room to read it. So they locked up and went to their rooms. Julia climbed into bed and thumbed through the pages until she arrived at poem VIII,

"Wretched Cattalus, you should stop fooling,

You know you've lost admit losing | The sun shone brilliantly for you, time was, when you kept following

where a girl led you, loved by us as we shall love no one, there when those many amusing things happened which you wanted nor did the girl not want . . . .now she's stopped wanting, you must stop . . . Don't chase what runs away nor live wretched but with a mind made up be firm, stand fast."

Julia closed the book and softly repeated, "don't chase what runs away . . . but with a mind made up be firm, stand fast." She now understood why her mother was not a coward because she did not fight for her father to stay, but she had made up her mind to stand fast and to not chase someone who no longer wanted to stay. She knew she would not question her mother again. She was seeing sides of her mother she never knew existed. Sides of her mother, she was sure her father may be a stranger to as well. She wondered how a person can live with someone their whole life with unrevealed facets of their personality.

THIRTEEN

N EW YORK WAS BLANKETED in snow. Julia and Ana flew in late. She was glad it was Sunday. She could stay in bed. Maybe get some writing done in the Writing Box. She reached for the box, set it on her bed and pulled out a scented unlined sheet of monarch size paper.

Dear Writing Box, so my parents are getting a divorce! I was in denial. But, not anymore. It's starting to feel real. Dad was not here when we got home last night. He moved out over the weekend. Even his writing shed looks just like a shed now. We heard he got an apartment in the city.

Mom seemed to take it in stride, no red puffy eyes. Maybe it's just me that has to get on board.

Is this something adults can just do? Like go back to a baseline of who they were before they were coupled? Is that even a thing? But I haven't developed a baseline. I am a creation of them. Ew! Skipping the biology of it all. Maybe I need to stop thinking my identity is all nature. How much of my personality is from the things I experienced? From my own personal perspectives? Maybe I can have a relationship with each of my parents separately. And love them—separately for who they are and not punish them for who they are no longer.

But I still feel un-whole somehow. Like I am no longer part of something. Dismembered. He broke our family. Does that make me, a member, broken too? I feel broken. In their eagerness to find their new normal and pick up the pieces of their lives, will they see me? Or just through me?

Julia massaged her temples. Fat tears made a slow descent down the pillows of her pink cheeks. She sniffed and brushed them away. Her stomach growled heralding the lack of breakfast. She smiled. Swung her legs off the bed and made her way to the kitchen.

"Hey sleepy-head, I just toasted an everything bagel. Want one?" Ana asked cheerily.

"Yes please. Can I have cream cheese on mine though?" asked Julia. As she watched Ana smear butter and jelly on her own.

Ana said, "sure honey."

They ate sitting around the kitchen island. A bright morning sun streamed through the white lace curtains. The bare trees outside wore thick coats of white powdery snow. Outside looked like an expanse of whiteness, purity and serenity.

"What's the plan for today?" Ana broke into Julia's thoughts.

"Not sure. What do you have in mind?" Julia asked.

"How about the mall, then some lunch after. Maybe Samantha would like to come too?" Ana suggested.

"I'm not sure. She's probably busy." Julia hedged, "but I'll shoot her a text and see."

Her mother seemed satisfied to drop it. Ana walked to the sink, pulled on rubber gloves and washed up the breakfast things. Julia finished her bagel and dropped her plate in the soapy water. "Just let me know when you're ready mom. I'm going up to my room to finish up some homework."

"Sure honey." Ana said.

"Hey Samantha" Julia texted. She was trying to figure out how to keep it casual. Something had happened between them, except she couldn't figure out what it could be. She just knew that Samantha was always over at her house, and now they barely speak although they have many of the same classes together and they're on the soccer team together, yet somehow, they kept missing each other.

It all started last summer after Samantha came back from Trinidad with Julia. Julia had invited Samantha and was thrilled when her parents said she could go with them. She was happy that her best friend and her grandmother got along. Samantha found it hard to always understand Jonathan and his sisters. She said their accents, especially Nalini's and Shoba's, were hard for her to always get it. Julia thought she would complain about the heat, because Samantha loved winter the best. But she didn't complain except for the first night.

If she was honest with herself she was getting annoyed towards the end with the way Samantha acted around Jonathan. She giggled at practically everything he said and Julia knows Jonathan is not that funny, although he did seem quite attentive. He would ask Samantha if she was thirsty or hungry.

Julia told herself nothing about his attentiveness bothered her so she couldn't understand why Samantha would suddenly start avoiding her. The only thing she could think of was when they came back to New York, Samantha had asked her for his number a couple of times, but Julia never gave it to her. Besides, she knew how busy Jonathan would be with exams coming up and that he was just being polite to her friend. She didn't think Samantha could be upset about that.

"Hey Julia. What's up?" Julia jumped when the phone dinged. She hadn't expected to get a text back. She had gotten accustomed to seeing her messages left on read.

"Nothing much. We're going to the mall. Wanna come?"

"Who's we?" Samantha texted

"My mom and I."

"When?"

"In a little while. When we're getting ready to leave, we could pick you up?" Julia texted

"I don't know. I got stuff to do," Samantha texted.

"Ok. I get it. See you at school then?" Julia ended the chat deflated.

"K."

Julia dropped her phone on her bed and walked to the bathroom to brush her hair and put it in a pony. After a little while, thinking at least she tried, her phone dinged. She thought it was her mom, texting her *"in 5"*, but it was from Samantha.

"I get it now . . ." Samantha texted.

Julia was confused. Did Sam text her by mistake. What was she talking about. What did she now get? *"Get what Samantha?"* Julia asked.

"You won't talk to me at school, in front of everyone. Is that why you're asking me to go to the mall, because you're ashamed I'm your friend. Or can I even use that word to define this relationship?" Samantha shot back.

"Wait what . . . what are you talking about. You're the one that's been avoiding ME!" Julia texted back. She knew using all caps meant you're angry. But she was or at least hurt and confused.

"Why don't you just be honest with me or at least with yourself Julia?" Samantha wrote.

"I am so confused. I honestly have no idea what you're talking about. Is this about Jonathan?" Julia asked.

"Hmm, funny you should bring his name up. Why would you think it was about him? Yes Julia it's about Jonathan. Why can't you be honest and tell me, your best friend, what's really going on between the two of you instead of me making a fool of myself thinking he likes me when he was just being polite because he LIKES YOU!" Samantha texted.

"I feel like such a fool. Throwing myself at him. You and he must have had a good laugh when I kept asking you for his number. Now I know why you kept making excuses about his strict parents, and his exams so you wouldn't have to give it to me," Samantha tapped not waiting for Julia to reply to the first message.

So that's what this was about. Julia's entire world is falling apart and Samantha thinks there is something going on between her and Jonathan. Yes, she did notice him in a different way last summer, and thinks he sees her differently too, especially this summer after the cricket match on the beach, but neither person has said anything to the other to confirm if these feelings are mutual.

"Look Sam, no one is laughing behind your back. There's nothing going on between Jonathan and I. I just didn't see how things can work with him living so far away and I didn't want you to get hurt. Besides, there is very little in my life these days to laugh about. Anyway, my mom is calling. I gotta go. TTYL." Julia tapped.

Samatha sent her a confused thinking emoji. Julia ignored it.

Julia and Ana spent an afternoon at the mall and then decided to go to the movies. They picked up Thai on their way home and had an early night.

The next morning, a pale sun peeped through

the dappled leaves. The school buses barreled down the street. She got dressed, made a sandwich for lunch and headed out the door. She saw Samantha sitting in her usual seat, third from the back on the left. She slid in beside her.

"Hey" Julia broke the ice.

"Hey" Samantha said. Then immediately she turned to face her with a look of concern. "What's that about *'there's very little in my life to laugh about'*. Jules what's going on?" Samantha asked.

"My parents are getting a divorce" Julia gushed out. Saying it to Samantha suddenly made her feel less alone.

"Not Peter and Ana" Samantha gasped. Julia nodded tears welling up in her eyes. "Oh Jules," Samantha cooed and pulled her close. "I've been such a bad best friend. I know there's nothing between you and Jonathan, or at least, nothing you guys have admitted to yourselves. I see you like the slow burn girl. He's hot. Just saying." They giggled. "But seriously how are you doing?" Samantha queried.

"Honestly, just taking it day by day. I'm going to my dad's this weekend for the first time. Glad we have a short week, not glad that's it's Thanksgiving weekend and we don't spend it all together. I guess there's going to be a lot of firsts in the near future.

Mom's decided to work for the holiday weekend." Julia explained.

"Well, listen, for what it's worth. I'm here for you. What happens the nights your mom has to work? You know you could stay at my house. I'd have to tell my parents though." Samantha asked.

"No, it's fine. Dad will come over. He wants to make things less disruptive as possible." Julia thanked her for the offer.

The bus pulled up at school. They filed out and headed to class.

The rest of the week Samantha and Julia were inseparable. They sat together during class, ate at lunch and spent the evenings at each other's house after school. Ana was glad to see some things go back to normal.

Thursday arrived and Peter pulled into the driveway to pick up Julia. Ana stood at the kitchen door to wave her goodbye. When Julia got in the car, Peter asked, "got everything?" She nodded.

Peter lived about forty-five minutes away. When they got to his building on East 76th Street, the doorman met them at the car to help Julia with her things. Julia looked up at the limestone façade and asked, "which floor is yours?"

"We are on the fifth floor," he replied.

They entered his apartment. It was a classic

six with a living room, full dining room, two bed-rooms, two and half bath, kitchen and library with parquet floors.

"You live here alone dad?" Julia asked peering inside the living room half expecting to see some-one there.

"Yes," he replied. "Are you hungry? Do you want a little snack before the big turkey dinner?"

"Sure, what you got?" Julia asked.

'I could make you a sandwich. Or if you would like a bowl of cereal to tide you over." Peter suggested.

'A bowl of cereal." Julia decided.

'So whose coming for Thanksgiving dinner? Or is it just us?" Julia casually asked.

"Do you want some fruit too?" Peter avoided answering the question.

Julia squinted her eyes at her father as if to ask, what are you not saying. Wait. He wouldn't dare. There's no way he's bringing that Maggie -editor person to dinner. He can't be. It's too soon.

"Do you remember my editor, Maggie Wess? Well she has a little boy named Harry and a twelve-old girl named Olivia. They've all heard so much about you and Olivia can't wait to meet you. I've invited them for Thanksgiving dinner. I hope you don't mind." Peter blurted careful to avoid meeting Julia's eyes.

"You can't be serious. You want me to meet the woman ruining my life." Julia gaped at her father appalled.

"Julia, I'm sorry you feel that way. But she happens to be the woman who makes me feel alive. It hurts me to hear you speak this way when you haven't even met her or given her a chance." Peter sounded bruised.

"Well I don't want to meet her or her two brats. What about mom?" Julia demanded, hot tears stung the corners of her eyes.

"Julia don't be unkind. I won't tolerate it," Peter scolded.

Julia needed to get away from this conversation and from him. She could no longer look at her father, this man, changed, standing in front of her, and keep a respectful tone. It was too much too soon. Did no one care how she was handling things?

She headed for one of the bedrooms. She would figure out which was hers when she got there. She heard her father follow behind her. "This conversation is not over. But let me show you to your room." Peter trailed behind. They entered a bedroom hallway. "It's the second door on the right," he directed.

She entered a square, dove-gray and white room with floor-to-ceiling drapes and an en suite bath. A large bed in the center with a white duvet and fluffy pillows. She saw her backpack in the closet. She reached for it and pulled out her headphones.

Her father sat at the foot of her bed with slumped shoulders. It was the first time she really took in the small changes in him over the past couple of months.

Julia was not oblivious, although Peter often was, to the stir he caused when he entered a room. Women's eyes followed him when he walked partly because he was tall, but partly because of the way he held himself. But the events of the last few months had taken its toll even if in subtle ways. Julia studied his face. He had shadows under his eyes. And although his beard was neatly trimmed, he needed a haircut. His shirt seemed a little loose than fitted.

"You are important to me Jules. And Maggie is important to me. I just want you to give her a chance. Get to know her, for me please?" Peter pleaded.

"What about mom?" Julia asked. She flung this question at every suggestion he made recently. It had become a reflexive, rhetorical question she relished.

Peter sighed. "What about your mom?"

"She wouldn't like it if I liked Maggie. It would seem like a betrayal. I don't need a mother. I have one. Don't try to make me like Maggie, dad." Julia declared.

"Jules, I would never ask you to do something against your principles. I am not asking you to like Maggie or replace her as your mother. No one can take your mother's place. I am asking you to treat her with respect and have an open mind about who she is as a person," Peter explained.

"Fine. But can we change the subject now? Will you be at my game next week? Or should I ask, is it your turn? It's getting hard to keep track of when you're supposed to be there or pick me up to see Dr. Jones for my braces, etc." Julia asked.

"I'm glad you mentioned that. Your mother and I discussed getting for us three," at the mention of 'us three' Julia broke out into a wide grin, Peter caught it but ignored it, "a subscription to the My Family app so we can have all your scheduled appointments and games on a digital calendar, so we're all on the same page. See, nothing will fall through the cracks, like I promised." He concluded with a flourish.

"My Family app. Huh! I like it. That's a good plan. I'll download it now," said Julia. "Look who's entering the 21st century," Julia giggled. "Okay, let's see how I can prevent you from making this Thanksgiving dinner a disaster." She rose to go to the kitchen and playfully chucked his shoulder on the way out.

"Elder abuse," Peter laughed and said.

FOURTEEN

I T WAS EVENING. The house smelled of pine-cones, but from the kitchen was the smell of baked ham and sweet potatoes. Julia was putting on a pair of stud earrings when her father said, "Julia they're here." She heard his footsteps in the foyer. Then the door open and the sound of a little boy.

She walked in to see him hoist a little cherubic boy onto his shoulders laughing. A tall brunette followed discreetly behind with a girl of about twelve beside her. Julia remained slightly out of sight watching the domestic scene play out before she announced herself. She wanted to watch them in their natural state. From the outside, they looked like a happy family.

Then Peter called for her again. 'Here goes' she thought.

"Maggie this is Julia. Julia this is Maggie Wells," her father made introductions.

Maggie put her hand out. Good start. Don't assume familiarity and seek a kiss. Julia politely shook it and said 'hi'.

"Well shall we sit to eat. I'm starved," Peter announced.

"Yes uncle Peter. I'm starved too," Harry said. He slipped his little chubby hands into Peter's as they walked to the dining room.

Maggie and Julia walked together, strides matching. "Your father tells me you play soccer." She said leaving it for Julia to pick up should she wish to. Julia simply nodded.

When they reached the dining room, Peter asked Julia if she could set the table. Immediately, Olivia volunteered to help too. Maggie asked if she could help Peter bring the dishes from the kitchen and he smiled sheepishly and said she could.

Julia watched her father interact with Maggie and her children. Harry clearly looked up to him like he was a superhero, and it was obvious he adored him. It never dawned on Julia that her father may have wanted a son. She always thought she was enough. But seeing how easily her father laughed out loud and how at ease he was with Harry and Olivia caused her to wonder if her father wanted a big family.

She watched Maggie too. She was different than Ana. She had a confidence and an assuredness in her very bearing that Ana lacked. Maggie took time and care with whatever she did. She sauntered slowly into the living room like a panther, found a single chair and lowered herself into it, enveloping all of it before crossing her long slender legs. Ana would plop onto a chair and curl her legs up under her as though always expecting to make room for someone else.

Maggie knew the power of her own beauty and its allure. She neither sought nor required validation from the male gaze that she was beautiful. When Peter complimented Ana, she would not meet his eyes but would look away embarrassed and uncomfortable, not Maggie. She possessed an inner knowing that she was elegantly and appropriately dressed for the occasion and therefore accepted compliments graciously.

Julia chided herself for making comparisons. Despite her best efforts, Julia had to admit she was a little fascinated by her and quite intrigued by her father's new mannerisms, or at least, new to her. She thought it might be true when people say that different people bring out different sides of you.

With Maggie around, he was more serious but not in a somber way, just less comical with more wit. This probably had to do with the fact that he knew Maggie would pick up on all his literary allusions and metaphors. It was clear they were both well read.

Ana was a serious person; some would even describe her as a little intense. Perhaps it had to do with the life and death nature of her profession. This was probably why Peter may have felt he needed to bring levity and humor to keep things balanced.

But with Maggie, Julia saw her father in another light. He seemed more in his element. He still commandeered the room, but Maggie as a person was less talkative than Julia thought for an editor. She mentioned as much during dinner. She was shocked at herself for expressing her thoughts so openly and early in the meeting, but Maggie's unassuming manner was disarming.

"I didn't realize editors can be so quiet," Julia commented.

"Why do you say that?" Maggie seemed genuinely curious.

"Well, the power of the red pen and all," Julia said off handedly.

"The power of the red pen. I've never quite heard it said that way before. Hmm. Do you write as well?" Maggie drew her out.

"Oh dad is the writer in the family." Julia deflected.

"Meaning there can't be more than one?" Maggie countered.

"Well, sure I guess. I just never saw myself as a writer. Although this summer, I think I might be becoming one." Julia said more to herself.

"Jules, what do you mean. What happened this summer?" Peter took the reins of the conversation.

"Well, grams gave me a writing box and I've been writing just little letters to myself. Nothing major," Julia said.

"A writing box. Julia that is amazing. Was it a family heirloom? I've only ever seen them in the museum. If you would permit me to, I would love to see it one day." Maggie stared at Julia in awe that she possessed such a piece of antiquity. Julia beamed.

"So, Perla decided to give you her papa Akash's writing box, huh, I wondered who she was going to pass it down too. You know I always secretly hoped it would be me," Peter confessed.

"What did you mean by the power of the red pen Julia?" Maggie asked. Julia was beginning to see why Maggie was a good editor. She also liked that Maggie did not assume a level of familiarity to call her Jules.

"Well it's just that dad is always saying the 'power of the editor's red pen can cut a man off at the knees'," Julia explained.

Peter purposefully avoided all eye contact. Maggie laughed a tinkling sound like a breeze passing through wind chimes.

"Good editors must first be good listeners. They use their red pen to cut through the brush to allow the writer to elevate his thoughts to reach new heights. Often writers need permission to get rid of the labyrinthine, tangled thoughts that's where the red pen comes in to allow thoughts that lead to writing that is clean, crisp and clear." Maggie explained.

Hooked, Julia asked, "how do you do that?"

"The challenge is to figure out if the writer needs the tools or the courage," Maggie said.

"Courage. But doesn't it already take courage to write?" asked Julia.

"Sometimes they need the courage to write about the things that are most difficult for them. Many writers only want to stay in the safe spaces and talk about feelings and ideas they have thoroughly processed, but not talk about the things that make them feel afraid or vulnerable." Maggie continued.

Despite Julia's earlier resolve to not like her, she had to admit she was forming a measure of respect for her.

"So Maggie what would you say dad needs?" Julia asked innocently.

Peter almost choked. He coughed and stared hard at Julia, the tips of his ears turned bright red. He sprang from his seat and headed for the kitchen.

Maggie did not follow him with her eyes. Her eyes fixed on Julia, she cooly replied, "I would say courage. Your father is a brilliant writer and understands when and how to use literary techniques. But he can also be self-effacing."

"Peter would you like any help?" Maggie asked. Ready to change the subject.

"No thank you. Why don't you and Harry get the Scrabble board set up? Julia and Olivia will help me clear the table. Right girls?" Peter asked as though he had asked 'the girls' to do this a thousand times. They nodded.

Maggie and Harry went to the living room as Julia carried the dishes to the sink and Olivia collected all the silverware. They worked quietly for a while. Julia caught Olivia looking at her a couple of times.

"Julia, are you like sixteen?" Olivia bravely asked.

"Almost. When do you turn thirteen?" asked Julia

"Next March. So far away," Olivia sighed.

'I used to feel like that at your age. Do you have a list?" Julia asked.

"A list. You mean of presents I want?" Olivia asked

"That kind too. You see, every year my mom and I would make a 'things you can do [at that age] list. Like when I turned thirteen, I could now paint my nails, get dropped off at the mall without parental supervision, that kind of thing," Julia explained.

"That's so cool your mom would do that with you. We don't have a list, we have just one item. When I turned twelve, I could stay up an hour longer so now my bedtime is 10pm instead of 9pm. But when I'm thirteen, my mom said I could go on work trips with her. I'm so excited about that one." Olivia said.

After the table was cleared and they helped stack all the dishes in the dishwasher, Julia and Olivia decided to join Maggie and Harry in the living room. They walked out of the kitchen and down the hall to the living room, when Julia felt a little hand slip into hers. She smiled.

In the living room, Maggie sat on the floor with Harry beside her. Peter sat cross-legged opposite them. The Scrabble board was open in front of them. There were four racks in four spots. Maggie was helping Harry so there were two open spots for each of them. Olivia and Julia sat across from each other.

"Great, now that everyone is here, the game can begin," Peter declared.

"Oh boy here comes the Kilmere competitive side!" Julia announced.

"Hey watch it. Where do you think you get it from when you're on the soccer field?" Peter retorted.

"'Dad, that's different. We're with family . . ." Julia caught herself. She can't believe how easily that slipped out her mouth. Was that telling? Did she really see Maggie and her children as part of her family?

"Julia you play soccer?" Maggie asked.

"Um, yeah," Julia replied.

"How do you like it?" Maggie continued.

"Fine," Julia said.

"I couldn't do sports in school. I just wasn't co-ordinated. So I settled for ballet. Not that it didn't have it's share of injuries, but at least I couldn't disappoint my teammates. You must hear this a lot, but do you know what you want to be when you grow up?" Maggie continued.

"I haven't much thought about it actually," Julia hedged.

"You have time," Maggie concluded.

After the Scrabble game, Maggie said it was getting late and they left. Peter rode in the elevator with them to walk them to their car. When he got back upstairs, he asked Julia if she wanted a cup of hot chocolate. She nodded.

"Dad, I'm just going to change into pajamas and come back out," Julia said.

When she came back to the living room, her father had also changed into lounge clothes. He brought two steaming cups of hot chocolate with marshmallows and set it on a nearby side table to cool.

"I want to hear how you enjoyed the evening?" Peter asked.

"You mean you want to know if I liked Maggie, Harry and Olivia?" Julia asked him from under her long eyelashes.

"Only if you want to. There is no pressure or expectation from me." Peter assured her.

"Well, I liked them. And I don't feel like I am betraying mom. I liked that Maggie didn't assume she already knew me, but just had a conversation with me. Olivia is sweet and Harry is adorable. But dad, does this mean every time I'm here, they will be here too?" Julia asked worried.

"Of course not. They are not always here," Peter said. But something in the way he said it made her think that although the kids are not always here, there was another member of the family that did come often. Julia decided she didn't want to know anymore.

"Want to watch a movie? It's still early," Peter suggested.

"Sure," Julia agreed stifling a yawn.

FIFTEEN

WHEN JULIA RETURNED home that evening from her dad's, her mother was in the kitchen heating up leftovers. She opened the back door and wiped her boots on the mat.

"Hey mom," said Julia.

"Hey honey. Glad you're home. How was your weekend?" asked Ana nonchalantly.

'It was good. Ate and ate. How was yours?" Julia asked.

'Worked and worked. I just got home a little while ago. Hey, I have next weekend off. I was thinking how about a day in the city. We could go shopping and then lunch in Central Park at the Boathouse? What do you say?" asked an excited Ana.

"Central Park—shopping—lunch—yes, yes!" Julia shrieked.

"Great. It's a plan. Oh by the way, your dad and I are meeting Mrs. Schroeder on Thursday for parent-teacher conferences. Anything we should know?" asked Ana

"No," Julia replied. Wracking her brains as to what might possibly come up that she needs to think up an excuse for. She knew her grades were not great this semester, but she didn't think she was failing so she wasn't worried too much.

"Hey mom, I have some homework to finish up. I'll come say good night when I'm ready for bed okay?" Julia suggested.

"Sure honey," Ana replied. Taking her soup and salad into the living room and turning on the television.

When Thursday came around, Peter and Ana drove separately to the school. They sat outside the classroom on a bench to wait their turn. Ana walked along the hallway looking at the students work on the wall. She spotted Julia.

"Here's Julia's!" she exclaimed.

Peter rose and walked over to peer at it. They stood silently watching the handiwork of their child. Proud parents. Then they heard, "Mr. and Mrs. Kilmere". They chorused a reply, "Here." They looked at each other and chuckled.

They walked into Mrs. Schroeder's classroom. It had a wall of windows on the east-facing wall, with a wall of lockers in the rear. Charts and maps lined the wall. Dioramas were in full display on a large rectangular table. A soft, square rug rested in a corner with two long bookshelves. Peter pulled out a book and frowned.

"How come everything is in German," he whispered to Ana.

"Because Mrs. Schroeder is the homeroom teacher and the German teacher," she whispered back.

"Peter and Ana. Thank you for coming in this morning. Have a seat," said Mrs. Schroeder.

Through the wall of windows, gray clouds hung low casting long shadows along the walls. Mrs. Schroeder switched on her desk lamp and opened a thick folder in front of her. She spent a few moments looking at it. Selected a few items and set them off to the side.

"I'm glad you both were able to make it in so we can have an opportunity to chat about Julia's work here this semester. Before we begin, has there been any significant changes at home I should know about?" asked Mrs. Schroeder.

Peter couldn't tell if this was a routine question, or if this was Mrs. Schroeder's way of giving them a chance to talk about things. While Peter collected his thoughts, Ana spoke up.

"Yes Mrs. Schroeder. There has been. A couple of months ago, Peter and I separated and in the process of getting a divorce," she said her voice even and steady.

"Julia lives primarily with her mother, but spends regular weekends with me or the nights Ana works," Peter piped in. He hoped he conveyed how involved he still was in Julia's life.

"That is a big change," Mrs. Schroeder said. Her eyes ping-ponged back and forth between them as she tried to digest the news. She had heard rumors but she would not listen to them until she heard from Peter and Ana herself. "Big change," she repeated more to herself. "Thank you for being candid. This now explains some of Julia's recent behavior." She saw the concern on their faces.

She pulled out one of Julia's recent German term papers. She got a C. Peter reached for it and tried to read some of it. It had been a while since he read German so he it took him a while to read a paragraph.

"Julia wrote this?" he asked incredulous.

Mrs. Schroeder nodded.

"But's it's full of run-on sentences and half completed thoughts. This is not like her," Peter concluded.

"I agree. This was a sample of the kind of work I have been getting from her. I know it's not like her, but when I asked her if everything was okay, she said everything was fine." Mrs. Schroeder explained.

"Mr. and Mrs. Kilmere, if I may, sometimes when I see children struggle at school when otherwise it would not be the case, it's because they are trying to find ways to cope with changes in their life. From what you told me, it now makes sense why Julia's grades dropped. Her focus shifted. They are resilient, but not emotionally equipped to cope in the same manner as adults. I am sure you have left the doors of communication open, but more may be needed," Mrs. Schroeder said.

Peter and Ana nodded their assent. "What do you recommend?" Ana asked.

"Talk to Julia. Check in with her regularly. Ask her how's she doing and just listen. It will reassure her of your love, it can validate her feelings and in turn make her feel more secure. She has become painfully aware what little control she has over her world whereas before she may have felt sure-footed. Now not so much. This level of uncertainty can cause stress and anxiety, and not always the visible kind," concluded Mrs. Schroeder.

"Yes we can certainly have more open conversations with Julia. Thank you Mrs. Schroeder," Peter reassured. They rose and left the parent-teacher conference. They walked out to the hallway together and saw Samantha's parents, Mr. and Mrs. Grotter. They exchanged greetings and headed to the parking lot.

Before they parted ways, Peter said, "Ana do you have time for us to grab some lunch and talk about that meeting with Mrs. Schroeder?"

"Yes, I do. Where do you have in mind?" asked Ana.

"We can go to the Town Home diner. We can walk to it," Peter said.

Ana nodded.

When they arrived, they were shown a booth against the back wall. The waitress came to take their drinks order. Her eyes lingered on Peter who was studying the menu. Ana looked up and just smiled.

He looked up and caught Ana's smile and re-flexively smiled back. Then swiveled his gaze to the waitress and said, "I'll have a hamburger cooked rare with a salad and a Coke. She'll have the Cobb salad and a glass of Perrier," he ordered. He snapped the menu shot and handed it to her with a wide grin.

"I'll make sure they get your order correct," the waitress purred never once looking at Ana. He nodded.

Ana shook her head and smirked.

"What's so funny?" Peter chided.

"You. You're just so oblivious. The poor waitress. Anyway, never mind. What do you think about what Mrs. Schroeder said?" asked Ana turning serious.

"I thought Julia was adjusting well, but I guess I was wrong. I definitely think it's worth having more open conversations with Julia. I just figured we're the type of parents that she could always come to us with anything that bothered her," Peter said and ran his fingers through his hair.

Ana sucked in her breath and peeled her eyes away from him. "I think we are that kind of parents, but like Mrs. Schroeder said, more is needed than keeping the lines of communication open. We need to initiate conversation that encourages Julia to tell us what she thinks and feels. I know I'm guilty of not having those conversations with her. I've been so caught up trying to process everything and not burden her, that I didn't realize I need to create a safe space for her to talk about her feelings, her fears and her concerns." Ana confessed.

Their order arrived. Peter tucked into his hamburger, then swiped his mouth with the napkin. Ana drizzled honey mustard dressing over her salad and mixed it in.

"I think the one-on-one approach is a good start," Peter said as he reached into Ana's plate to spear a cherry tomato, his favorite, off her plate. Ana froze but did not say anything.

"I also think I want to have my chat with her outside the house. We're planning to go to Central Park on Saturday. We'll talk then," said Ana.

"Are you planning to have lunch at the Boathouse?" Peter asked.

Ana nodded.

"The weather should be nice for a walk around the pond. Remember that time, we rented one of the gondolas," Peter smiled and asked.

Ana was not prepared to go down memory lane. "Co-parenting is not easy for sure," she said.

Peter agreed. "I think I'll stop by the library this weekend and check out some books on children and divorce."

They fell into silence as they ate. When they were finished, Peter picked up the check and Ana thanked him for lunch. They walked back to school and parted ways at the parking lot.

SIXTEEN

ON SATURDAY, JULIA and Ana decided to drive into the city instead of taking the train from Everly. It was a cool, dewy morning. They found a spot on Park Avenue and walked down to Lexington and 59th Street to Bloomingdale's.

They browsed the make-up section and then went up to the shoe floor. At around 11:30a.m they headed up Fifth Avenue to make their way to lunch at the Loeb Boathouse in Central Park. When they arrived, they were seated inside with an unobstructed view of the pond.

It was called the boathouse because the Victorian structure was first used to store canoes. Over the years, it was transformed into a restaurant boasting a dining room, bar and a wall of windows overlooking the pond.

"You know dad doesn't live far from here," Julia mentioned.

"Really. Do you want him to join us?" Ana asked suddenly looking nervous.

"No, just saying that's all," Julia said.

The waiter appeared. "What would you like?" he chirped.

"I'll have the tuna nicoise," Ana said.

"And I will have the Boathouse Burger and fries please," Julia ordered.

"And to drink?" asked the waiter.

"Waters with lemon wedges please," Ana said.

"I'm so glad we came here. It's so pretty even in the winter with the bare trees," said Julia.

"I'm glad we can spend this time together. No housework, no homework, or projects, just be, you know," Ana said. She took a deep cleansing breath.

Julia smiled, "same," she said.

Their order arrived. They laid their cloth napkins on their laps and waited for him to leave.

"May I ask you something?" Ana began.

"Sure mom. What's up?" Julia said and took a bite.

"These last few months, our family has gone through some changes. I just wanted to ask, how are you doing?" she asked as she pierced a boiled egg with her fork and brought it to her mouth.

Tears sprang up in Julia's eyes. She wasn't

expecting this. She stared at the gondolas for some time. "It's been so hard mom," Julia sniffed. She did not want to cry in public. "I know it's not your fault, but I feel so alone."

A sociable blue jay landed on the black railing in front of them. He cocked his head and looked at her. She smiled. Ana reached across and stroked her forearm to encourage her to speak if she wanted to, that she was here to listen.

"Do you remember a couple of weeks ago, I was working on a project for school on the fractal patterns in nature and the Golden Ratio for Ms. Kelly's science class?" asked Julia.

Ana bobbed her head up and down.

"Well, I learned about the nautilus," said Julia.

"The not-often seen sea creature," Ana asked. She wanted to be sure she could follow.

"Yes. I feel like a nautilus. Not-often seen," Julia said in a low voice.

'In what way?" Julia gently prodded.

"I think my coach sees a good athlete. My teachers see a good student, dad sees a good daughter, and possibly a good sister to a little girl . . ." she immediately glanced up to catch the pain that crossed Ana's eyes and bit her lips wishing she could take back the last phrase. But that was also it. She was busy trying to protect her mother's feelings. Why does that always happen? When one parent moves on and the other does not, the child may feel like they ought to protect the vulnerable parent.

Ana redirected the conversation back to the nautilus.

"Yes, like I was saying. All people probably see is a beautiful mollusk with all those swirls or sides to it. But it can also completely withdraw inside its shell and close down the hood so to speak. People don't know that can happen," Julia cried.

"Honey, do you feel as though the real Julia has withdrawn insider her shell?" Ana gently asked.

Julia sniffed into her napkin and nodded unable to speak.

"Mom, I think I have. I've been shutting Samantha out. She always thought we were the perfect family. Funny, I thought so too. I don't know how to tell her we're not," Julia admitted.

"Maybe it's because you're still working out how to tell yourself," Ana said and paused.

Julia took a deep breath. "But we were at one time, weren't we mom," Julia needed to know if her secret was real for part of her life. She couldn't have made the whole thing up this whole time. She couldn't bear it, if it was all a lie.

"Sweetheart, we never were perfect. No family is. But it doesn't mean you didn't have a loving family. And still do. Isn't that what counts?" Ana asked.

Julia sat with that for a while as they finished their meal. Ana paid the bill and they walked out the restaurant to take a stroll towards the Bethesda Fountain. They found an empty wrought-iron park bench and sat.

Julia turned to her mother and asked, "Mum, what do you see when you look at me? Who do you see?"

"Hmm, there are two answers when you ask a mother that question. There is the mom answer and there is the individual's. The mom answer, I see my little girl and I want to protect her from every sad thought and feeling. The individual, I see a young woman who I admire and feel lucky to spend time and space with her. I am interested and curious about the things that make her happy, excited and worried. Not to fix it, but as a way of getting to know her more. As one person to another, I see someone whose interior world is changing, expanding beyond the family we started to include other people in that definition. And it is up to you to decide who you will let enter your world, who you will include or exclude from your definitions of close friends and family," Ana concluded.

Julia wrapped her arms around her mother's

lithe frame. They sat like that together until they started to shiver. Then laughed and walked arm in arm back to the car.

As they drove down Lexington Avenue, Ana spotted Alice's Tea Cup.

"Let's have tea and something scrumptious to go with it, shall we?" Ana asked with a mischievous twinkle in her eye. Julai giggled, "yes!"

They pulled over, parked and walked over to the cozy duplex café. They stepped inside.

When the hostess appeared, Ana asked, "table for two -upstairs please?"

When they were seated, Ana ordered a big slice of chocolate cake with thick, mint green frosting and two forks. Earl Grey tea for her and hot chocolate with whipcream for Julia. They giggled like schoolgirls. They rubbed their cold hands together blowing into them to warm them. The wind had turned blustery cold outside. But inside the cozy café, all was right in the world in that moment.

After their treat, they rushed back to the car and headed home as a light snow fell.

That night, after a long soak in the tub, Julia got into her pajamas and reached for her writing box. She pulled out a sheet of scented unlined paper. She rested her head against the headboard reliving her wonderful day. With thoughts converging, colliding and tumbling one into the other, she took a deep breath and tried to find order.

Dear Writing Box, I got it. I finally figured out what grams was about to tell me the night she left to help auntie Kavita. She was trying to tell me, 'I am the only one that could ever be ME!' That means I choose my definition for family and I decide who makes up my family. I thought it had to include only the people re-lated to me, but it can include the people who care about me, people who respect me and who I respect.

That goes for the rest of my inner world. I am not just the label others assign to me—stu-dent, soccer player, best friend, big sister, girl-friend—wait -cringe! Never mind, I see me, and I know those that love me will see me for me too! I don't have to just show the world my outside beauty but let people in to see my inner beauty too. And it's my inner beauty that makes me unique. Each one of us in the world unique and worthy of love.

"Julia, Julia! Hurry get dressed!", her mother yelled. Her voice sounded high and screechy like a mountain climber losing oxygen.

Julia scrambled out of bed and rushed to the top of the stairs. Her mother was panting at the bottom like she had been running.

"It's your father. He was in an accident. We're leaving for the hospital now. Hurry get dressed. I'll meet you in the car," Ana ordered. Julia obeyed.

SEVENTEEN

———

JULIA GOT IN THE CAR. She barely closed the door when Ana was already pulling out the driveway. "Mom, what happened to dad?"

"I don't know the details Jules. Once we get to the hospital, I'll know more," Ana said.

Julia did not know her mother knew how to drive above sixty-five miles per hour. But when she peeked over, they were doing eighty-five.

They pulled into the hospital's parking lot and rushed into the hospital lobby. Ana immediately headed for the emergency room and told Julia to sit in the waiting room while she checked if Peter was there.

He was not in the ER. But Ana found out he was in surgery and will be in room 302 when he gets out. They took the elevator to the third floor and made their way to the waiting room.

Ana walked behind the nurse's station to check the log of when he arrived and what was the initial diagnosis that made them go into surgery. After some time, she came back and found Julia.

"So dad was brought in because he was apparently hit by a driver when he was on his bicycle. So he's actually not in surgery but running scans and tests to make sure nothing is broken. He has a nasty cut on his left leg so he will need stitches. That's all we know for now. We can wait here or in his room, what would you like to do?" Ana asked.

"We can wait here. In case someone comes," Julia suggested. Ana nodded, "Okay. I"ll just be over here talking to the nurses. I'll be back in a little while."

While Ana was gone, Maggie showed up. She rushed over and gave Julia a hug. "How's your dad, Julia? Any news?" Maggie asked.

"They're running tests on him right now. Mom is here so she will let us know more soon." Julia reported.

"Oh your mom is on duty this evening?" Maggie was shocked.

"No, I think the hospital called her. We were home, so we came over. We just got here," said Julia.

Ana walked back in. Then jerked to a stop when she saw Maggie sitting next to Julia. She looked as though someone had slapped her in the face. She collected herself and walked slowly to Julia. "They're moving him to his room now," she said to no one in particular.

"Ana, I'm so sorry. If you need me to leave, I'll leave," said Maggie.

Ana shook her head. "No, it's fine," she said barely making eye contact.

They walked to Peter's room but Ana hung back and allowed Julia and Maggie to enter first. She came in after them, picked up his chart and focused on what she found there.

Peter sat up in bed with a wide grin looking devilishly handsome even with three stitches across his eyebrow, "hi guys!" His face softened when he saw who was at the foot of his bed studying his chart. "Hi Ana," he said softly.

She briefly met his eyes and smiled.

"How's it looking doc," he teased her.

She glared at him and he laughed. "Why don't you tell us in your words what happened?"

"Well instead of my usual run this morning, I thought I would bike to the park. Then out of nowhere, this car shot of a side street and bam! Slammed into me. I know I was thrown. I must have hit my head on the island I think because I blacked out. Next thing, I woke up here," Peter explained. He twisted and his face contorted in pain.

"No sudden moves, please," Ana instructed.

"Can they give him something for the pain?" Maggie pleaded.

"Yes, in a little bit. We need him lucid to make sure there was no concussion. Let's see what the test results say first," she answered.

"Ana can you wait outside for just a moment please?" Peter asked. Ana looked hurt but stepped outside.

"Maggie there is something that Ana and I would like to discuss with Julia. Thank you for coming, but I should be released today. Can we speak later when I get home this evening?" Peter asked.

Maggie nodded, "of course, I understand. I'll see you back at the apartment. I'll pick up some soup," Maggie offered.

"Thank you," said Peter. Then he turned to Julia, " can you ask your mother to come back in please?" Julia hopped off his bed and opened the door. She poked her head outside to find her mother pacing. "Mom, dad is asking for you," said Julia.

With them both there, Peter began, "Julia since we're all here, I thought this would be as good a time as any while we're waiting for labs and test results, to talk about a few things." Julia nodded in agreement, bracing herself.

"Jules I want you to know, to hear it from me, I love you very much. And I did not want to pressure you or force you to accept anyone in your life you don't feel comfortable with. My primary concern is you and what is best for you," his gaze pivoted to look at Ana, "your mother and I both feel that way."

A nurse walked in to look at his monitor and take his blood pressure. Then Dr. Wallace came in and said the CT scan showed no broken bones. Everyone breathed a sigh of relief. Ana walked out with him to ask more detailed questions.

"Looks like Dr. Kilmere is on duty," Peter winked. Julia chuckled. But seizing the opportunity of being alone, Peter said, "I'm glad we're alone. I said what I said earlier because Jules, I want you to know if I pushed you to meet Maggie and the kids too soon, I apologize. I should have given you more time."

Julia rose and walked to look out the window. "It's not that dad, it's just seeing you with them, I wondered if I was not enough. You looked so happy with her kids. It made me think is that why you left? You wanted more kids and mom didn't? Was that it?"

"No, it was not. Yes, I wanted a big family and your mother didn't, but there were other grown-up reasons. Julia, you are more than enough. But with love, there is always room to include others, no? How do you feel about being a big sister? Truly feel?" Peter asked.

"I don't know dad. I've never been one. Harry is adorable so I don't think I would mind, but I don't really want to think about that now. Maybe not while you're in a hospital."

"You're right. We'll drop the topic for now. But know this, whether there is a Harry or an Olivia in my life, no one can replace you. You're my first-born. That will never change. You will always hold a special place in my life." Peter declared.

"You mean that dad, really?" Julia felt like a huge weight had lifted off her shoulders. A psychological weight she did not even know she had been carrying. But now hearing those words from her father, reassured her. Bolstered her. She realized she is not losing her parent to another family, but growing her family.

EIGHTEEN

P
ETER WAS DISCHARGED from the hospital that evening. Julia rode with him in the taxicab to his apartment. Maggie, Harry and Olivia were there waiting for him.

Julia was happy to see them. She was happy to see her father so loved. She saw the Scrabble board and laughed. After they ate dinner, she sat on the floor with Harry and Olivia to play a game of Scrabble while Maggie set Peter up on the sofa to rest. Throughout the evening, she couldn't help notice how attentive Maggie was going back and forth for extra pillows, socks or extra blanket. She made chamomile tea for him and hot cocoa for the kids. Julia knew her father loved all the fuss. Around nine o'clock Ana picked up Julia.

When she got home, she took a shower and climbed into bed bone tired. She reached for the writing box. Then sat for a long-time giving orders and adjectives to her thoughts. After some time, a sense of calm came over her. When she reflected on the time with her mother in Central Park, the conversation with her dad at the hospital, her heart felt wider, happier and lighter than it had in months.

She remembered the conversation about the nautilus and how, like the nautilus with its hidden chambers of inner beauty, how often people just see the outer beauty and think that's all there is. But like the nautilus we all have hidden chambers of inner beauty. We must take the time to discover those hidden parts and not be quick to conclude that all there is to see is what we see on the outside. Each of us is so much more. All it takes is more curiosity and less judgement. She was ready to pen her next entry.

Dear Writing Box, I've been through many changes these past months. I never imagined you would be the keeper of my secrets, fears and hopes. After grandma's accident, my parents' divorce, and news that my family is expanding, perfect no longer looks one way.

I came face-to-face with new and at times uncomfortable feelings. There were times I was not proud of how I reacted and how much it was because I was scared. I was scared of how it would change me. But I realized that I like the changes it made in me. I grew as a person. I liked the process of writing it down. It helped me to gain perspective when I returned to that version of myself and read what I wrote. The times between the experience, the recording and the reviewing helped me to discern the growth. This exercise also helped me to see that not only my perspective has value but other people's as well. Thank you for the opportunity to chronicle my past self to help me meet my future self. Until the next entry.

THE END

THE CONVERSATION

A Forbes article[1] on divorce (Bieber, 2024) stated that "43% of first marriages ended in divorce . . . [and] when children are involved the divorce process also becomes more complicated . . .".

One may argue that to dissolve a marriage is a deeply personal matter. And it is. But at what cost to the child? The child who is the un-consulted, observant casualty of the dismantling of the marriage. A union which represented safety and security for that child; terms that will now come to mean something entirely different to them. This is the conversation I propose we have. This book offered a glimpse into a child might go through. It is my hope that it allows for more awareness of the emotional landscape of the child. And that this awareness, prompts support and opportunities for

---

1   "Revealing Divorce Statistics in 2024" by Bieber

open communication between parent and child in age appropriate ways.

We will explore this topic through the lens of the character, Julia.

1. The secret - the book begins with Julia's secret. She called it an 'inner-knowing she possessed' where she believed her life was perfect. She formed this belief because her parents were together and offered her a sense of safety and security. By the end of the book, do you think she believed her life was no longer 'perfect' since her parents were no longer together?

2. The announcement - what do you think of the way Peter and Ana chose to announce the news of their divorce to Julia? Would you have done something different?

3. Open spaces – Julia recognized in herself that her reaction to the news was different from theirs. She was angry and ready to explode while they calmly sat there looking at her. She needed to get away from them. She had the emotional maturity to understand that they had time to come to terms with the news while she was just hit with it. Do you

think this emotional distance made her feel 'separate and apart' from her parents at that moment? Do you think they created the write space for her to freely express how she felt? Ask her questions? Why or why not?

4. Processing and coping – Adhari Perla, Julia's grandmother gives her a gift from the past, a writing box. Do you think it helped Julia to process and cope with her feelings through the act of writing down her thoughts as a way of chronicling and preserving them in the box helped her to cope? What other mechanisms could she have used to derive the same bene-fits? Laptop? Journal?

5. Support - Do you think Ana, Julia's mother, was there for her emotionally and physically? Emotional support in the sense of creating opportunities for open conversation, possibly explanations and validations. Physical support in terms of just being there, approachable and accessible for Julia to not feel alone in this?

6. Statistics have shown that often the primary parent is the mother, and the visiting parent is the father. This was the case in this book.

Do you think Peter played enough of an active role in Julia's life? Did he keep his promise to her?

7. Moving on – how did Peter show sensitivity or insensitivity to Julia's feelings when Maggie and her children were invited to dinner?

8. School – at the parent-teacher meeting Ana and Peter seemed shocked to learn that Julia was struggling academically. Do you think this is because Julia hid it so well or could they have been more proactive to make sure she had the support she needed?

9. Co-parenting –do you think Julia felt both parents were present in her life or she was just shuttled between them?

10. Family – do you think towards the end of the book Julia came to like or respect Maggie for who she was? Do you think Julia re-defined family to include others beyond her biological father and mother? Should she?

ACKNOWLEDGMENTS

I want to thank my family and friends for their invaluable support. Thank you to Whitney Rodriguez for your help to better describe and explain the local Trini dishes. My sincere gratitude to my beta readers. Audria Brayboy for spending your Sunday evenings with me as a listening ear and sounding board. Jonathan Stephen, Deseree and Jonathan Maes for your critique and comments which helped me to stay true to my vision and strengthened the narrative.

Special thanks to Julie Scheife and Molly Mortimer at Mayfly Design for transforming my bundle of papers into what you now hold in your hand.

Sincere gratitude to The Alma Jordan Library, the West Indiana and Special Collections Division of The University of the West Indies, St. Augustine, Trinidad for their help with historical records on indentureship.

Finally, to my daughter, Jillian for inspiring me to write this book.